TANGO

TANGO

The Tale of an Island Dog

EILEEN BEHA

SCHOLASTIC INC.
New York Toronto London Auckland
Sydney Mexico City New Delhi Hong Kong

ISBN 978-0-545-23505-1

Copyright © 2009 by Eileen Beha.
All rights reserved. Published by Scholastic Inc.,
557 Broadway, New York, NY 10012, by arrangement with
Bloomsbury USA Children's Books. SCHOLASTIC and associated logos
are trademarks and/or registered trademarks of Scholastic Inc.

12 11 10 9 8 7 6 5 4   11 12 13 14 15/0

Printed in the U.S.A.   40

First Scholastic printing, February 2010

Book design by Donna Mark

To Ralph. *Always.*

CONTENTS

PROLOGUE

The tale of a little dog named Tango takes place on an island, cradled by waves, in the Gulf of St. Lawrence.

It is a peaceful province where the sea laps against sandstone cliffs, bays and inlets offer quiet shelter for pairs of blue heron, and red clay roads wind like ribbons across rolling hills.

A bountiful island where potato vines bloom into white stars, purple lupine line the ditches, and rose red fireweed sparkles along fence lines.

A magical land where around every corner you glimpse the sea.

Named Abegweit by the people of the First Nations, this crescent-shaped island has a legend. Here, a soul will discover his true kindred spirit.

A legend not only about humans, mind you—but about all God's creatures, from the smallest of sea urchins to the strongest of shiny black seals.

And dogs?
Dogs, too, you ask?
But of course.

CHAPTER 1

Cold Creek Kennel

Early one morning, when the winds of March were raw and unrelenting, inside a puppy pen on George Bailey's farm, a Yorkshire Terrier named Sadie was sleeping on her side. Four puppies lay curled against her belly, like little boats anchored in a safe cove.

When she awoke, Sadie said to herself, "It's time." She nudged her puppies, nuzzling each leathery black nose. "It's time."

The puppies perked their ears, thinking that Mr. Bailey had brought in their breakfast.

Years ago, when Sadie was a very young mother, she'd blessed each newborn in her litter with a name.

But after Mr. Bailey sold her first three litters, Sadie stopped naming her offspring, and who can blame her?

Year in and year out, as soon as Sadie's puppies were weaned, Mr. Bailey scooped them up and trucked down to Boston, where he sold the litter for twice the price any small town pet shop owner would pay.

However, this spring, weeks had passed, and her four precious puppies were still by her side. Perhaps Sadie's prayers had been answered, and her son and three daughters would live out their lives at Cold Creek Kennel.

Now, Sadie placed her paw on the forehead of the largest female puppy. "I will name you Esperanza. May you bring hope and light to those who have lost their way."

To the second-largest female, Sadie said, "I will name you Theresa, for you will give generously to those in need."

By this time, the male puppy's mind was filled with wild imaginings. He thought about the tales his mother had told them of their fearless ancestors, the brave terriers of Yorkshire, who cleared rats out of shafts before coal miners entered with shovels and picks.

"Maybe she'll name me Sir Rex," he whispered to his unnamed sister.

He sat up straight and tall. "Or Apollo."

He puffed out his chest. "Or Zeus."

His sister howled with laughter.

At that very moment, Mr. Bailey opened the door to the kennel area.

Sadie, who didn't hear Mr. Bailey's footsteps, raised her paw, calling for silence. "I will name you Dulcinea. Wherever you go, joy and sweetness will follow."

The male puppy stood at attention. His docked tail quivered. His mother's paw was a royal scepter pointed to the sky.

"And you, my son, I name you—"

Suddenly Sadie's eyes widened. Her paw dropped. Mr. Bailey reached into the puppy pen and clamped the scruff of the male puppy's neck. The puppy squealed, a futile plea for release.

With a flick of his wrist, Mr. Bailey slid the trembling puppy into a plastic travel crate.

Esperanza, Theresa, and Dulcinea met the same fate.

As the imprisoned puppies rode off in the back of Mr. Bailey's van, Sadie pawed at the pen's steel bars until she was limp with exhaustion. The sound of Sadie's howls twisted around the rocky hills. Even Mr. Bailey's sheep stopped grazing in sympathy.

Inside the van, the puppies howled, too.

A few miles outside of Boston, George Bailey finally pulled his minivan over to the side of the road. He spun around in his swivel seat and shook his fist at the wailing puppies.

"Shut up!" he snarled, drawing a straight finger across his throat. "Or else!"

The four puppies huddled even closer together.

"I want Mama," Dulcinea sobbed.

"Shush," the male puppy admonished, "or he'll skin us alive for sure."

Now, what Sadie didn't know was that Mr. Bailey thought that this particular litter was her finest. Under wisps of glossy gold hair, the puppies' brown eyes sparkled. Their ears were fringed with feathers of golden fur as delicate as goose down. Their coats were charcoal gray and thick. They were strong-legged and spunky, destined to be champions.

In fact, the litter of Yorkshire Terriers was so fine that Mr. Bailey decided to bypass Boston. He drove straight south to New York City, where Esperanza, Theresa, Dulcinea, and their nameless brother were certain to bring top dollar.

CHAPTER 2

Paws 'n' Claws Pet Boutique

The owner of Paws 'n' Claws Pet Boutique on Manhattan's Upper East Side didn't hesitate for a moment when he heard George Bailey's asking price for the four Yorkshire Terrier puppies.

If the truth be told, breeds of dogs were like fashion in New York City: "in" one season and "out" the next. That season, Yorkies were "in."

After being displayed in the pet shop window only a few hours, the three female puppies had been sold.

With every last wave of a beloved sister's paw, the male puppy's tiny heart shrank. He turned his back on customers who ogled him. He growled at a teenage girl who examined him like he was secondhand merchandise. He bit a loutish boy with braces who tossed him around like a football.

At six o'clock, the owner of the pet shop turned off the lights. A door slammed. The puppy heard the click of a key turning in a lock.

Dusk turned into darkness. The bubbling aquarium cast eerie blue green lights overhead. A parrot named Ray talked in his sleep. Kittens cried. Dogs whimpered. Fear gripped the Yorkie by the throat, a choke chain that grew tighter with each passing hour.

The next afternoon, a tall woman and her fiancé strolled into the pet store. She pushed a pair of sunglasses to the top of her head and swept back waves of honey brown hair that tumbled over the collar of her trench coat. The man adjusted the gray cashmere scarf he'd tossed casually around his neck.

The pet shop owner rubbed his palms together. Such wealth, such privilege the pair radiated. His smile beamed as the woman fondled the Siamese kittens and the man scratched a Rottweiler puppy's ears. Acting on a hunch, the shop owner slyly placed a new price tag on the pen in which the Yorkshire Terrier was displayed.

A few minutes later, when the woman smiled down on him, the lonely little Yorkie couldn't bring himself to turn his back. Eyes glistening, the two-pound puppy jumped up and down against the bars of the cage. He balanced on his two hind legs and spun until his body toppled.

"Oh, look, Diego," the woman said. "He's dancing."

The man called Diego raised one eyebrow. "You call that a dog?"

The woman nuzzled the puppy's furry frame against her cheek.

Diego scrunched his nose. "There are rats in this city twice his size." He rubbed his hand over the day-old growth on his chin. "No—three times his size. They could eat him for lunch."

"We'll put him in private school," countered the woman in a teasing tone of voice. "Please, Diego—please? I love him already."

What could Diego do? The little dog had won the woman's heart.

An hour later, the woman, whose name was Marcellina, and Diego, burdened with bags of pet supplies, emerged from Paws 'n' Claws.

Horns blared, city buses grumbled, taxi drivers squawked, and tires squealed. Inside a fancy plaid pet carrier, the puppy trembled.

"Diego, I've decided," Marcellina announced as they crossed Madison Avenue.

"You've decided what?"

"His name," Marcellina said. "We'll call him Tango."

"Like the dance?"

"Like the dance."

Not surprisingly, the tango was the "in" dance step that season.

Tango? What about Rex—or Zeus? the puppy wanted to ask. Have you considered Apollo? Or Spike?

"Marvelous," Diego agreed. "Tango it is."

The little dog now known as Tango groaned. What would his mother think if she knew that he had been given such a silly name? His ears burned; he could almost hear his sisters laughing at him.

And so it was that Tango made a vow: somehow, some way, *someday* he would bring honor to his name.

Whining, he scratched on the carrier's mesh door. Diego unzipped the flap and tumbled Tango into the crook of Marcellina's arm.

Hordes of humans hustled past. Tango looked up, down, and all around. Where were the trees? Where was the grass?

"I know!" Marcellina said, pointing to an expensive jewelry store. "Let's go here!"

"Why? I just bought you a twenty-four-carat dog," grumbled Diego.

"No, silly. Not for me—for him." She squeezed

Diego's hand. "Tango has to have an identification tag. A silver heart would be lovely, don't you agree?"

Knowing that it would be futile to protest, Diego nodded. "And a silver collar, too, no?"

"But of course," replied Marcellina.

CHAPTER 3

The Lap of Luxury

Almost three years later, on a drizzly afternoon, Tango strained against a pearl-studded leather leash, gripped by his personal dog walker. Tango had finished his daily walk through Central Park and was eager to get home to Marcellina's apartment building, where the dark-suited doorman would give him a treat. After that, Tango planned to take a delicious nap on a willow green silk chaise lounge, custom-made to his size.

Once inside, Marcellina removed Tango's yellow hooded raincoat and four candy apple red boots.

She was bubbling with excitement.

"Squiggle-butt, I have fabulous news! Diego's birthday is two weeks from tomorrow. We—you and I—are going to give him the best birthday party ever. And when I say the best, I mean THE BEST."

Marcellina tapped Tango's snout. "But don't you tell him. It's a surprise."

With one exception—the sound of Marcellina unzipping an empty suitcase to pack for a trip—Tango loved surprises. And today, his mistress had a second surprise: Marcellina *herself* was going to give him his bath.

"The people from Suds 'n' Scissors can't make it today, Poochie-pie," she explained.

Soon Tango was soaking in bubbles that smelled like exotic calla lilies in bloom. His mistress massaged him with gentle fingers, rinsed him with lukewarm water, and toweled him dry. After she blow-dried his coat, Marcellina curled the steel blue strands into fluffy waves.

Even before Tango was dry behind his ears, Conrad—designer of couture fashions for Manhattan's most discriminating dogs—arrived.

Conrad ran a tape measure from neck to tail along Tango's spine. "Twelve inches," he murmured, marking his notepad.

He wound the tape around Tango's neck, chest, and midsection. "Nine, eleven, twelve—perfect!"

With a ruler, he measured Tango's legs. "Seven inches." He smiled. "Simply perfect!"

⬧

By seven o'clock on the night of Diego's birthday, Marcellina's penthouse was ablaze with black candles. Outside the glass walls, the cityscape glowed and glittered. Every time Marcellina opened the door, Tango ran in circles, barking with delight and wagging his stump of a tail—as much as a tail stump can waggle.

The champagne-sipping guests declared that the seafood buffet was *amazing.* The mermaid ice sculpture was *exquisite.* And Tango? Tango was *so-o-o-o precious* in his black tuxedo that he soon had a headache from all the ladies with long red fingernails patting him on the head, marveling, "Precious . . . simply precious."

Later, when a Latin dance combo played the first sultry notes of a tango, Marcellina lifted Tango up in her arms.

"They're playing our song," she whispered.

Marcellina's violet blue eyes sparkled like the sea on a sunny day as she rocked Tango around the room. Inside his heart, the love Tango felt for his mistress did its own kind of dance. Later, and for a long, long time to come, Tango would remember this moment and long for it.

The music stopped. Applause erupted. Breathless and beaming, Marcellina lowered Tango to the floor.

Without Marcellina's attention, Tango soon tired of Diego's birthday party. With each passing minute, the laughing, chattering guests seemed taller, bigger, louder. The gigantic, partying people bounced above Tango like the balloons he once saw in the Macy's

Thanksgiving Day parade. Tango wished they'd pop and go home.

Bored and hungry, Tango wiggled through a maze of pointy-toed pumps with spike heels, consuming every cracker crumb, crab lump, and cube of cheese he could find. He even devoured two olives out of an empty martini glass, but then felt woozy.

Somehow, he made his way to the top of the circular staircase. Pressing his muzzle between his paws, he peered through the railing and watched the spectacle below. Sometimes, Tango had to admit, he felt alone in this human world, where humans said, and did, things he didn't understand.

Tango was just drifting into an uneasy sleep when Diego exclaimed in a booming voice, "A sailboat! You bought me a sailboat? Marcellina, my sweet, my dear—my very own sloop! You're amazing!"

☙

A few days later, Tango sat primly on a brocade dining room chair, awaiting a slice of beef tenderloin. Around his neck, he wore his shiny silver link collar and a heart-shaped identification tag.

Soon, Tango realized, Marcellina and Diego were arguing. "I hate to disagree, DEAR," Marcellina said, "but I think it's too early to sail that far north. It's only April. I remember Father saying . . ."

"Nonsense, my dear," Diego countered. "Your

15

father lacks a spirit of adventure. What I need—what we need—is a challenge. Man against the sea and all that: Erik the Red, Christopher Columbus, Ahab—Ulysses!"

Adventure? Maybe Diego was onto something. . . . Maybe what Tango needed in his life was some adventure! Dog against the sea, and all that.

As fate would have it, Marcellina lost the argument.

Early on a warm, sun-filled April morning, Tango, Marcellina, and Diego traveled north to Maine where they made preparations for the maiden voyage of Diego's new sailboat. They would be sailing up the coast of Maine to Nova Scotia, around Cape Breton, and through the Cabot Strait into the Gulf of St. Lawrence.

At the marina, Tango pirouetted with pleasure, eager to set sail. That is, until—*whoops!*—he stepped dangerously close to the edge of the pier. In the dark, menacing water below, a whiskered fish stared up at Tango with a sinister grin.

Tango's heart went *ker-plunk*. What was he getting himself into?

Sporting a gold-braided captain's hat, Diego handed Marcellina a towel-wrapped bottle of champagne.

Into the gusty winds Marcellina shouted, "In the

name of all who have sailed the seas in the past, and all who will sail aboard this vessel in the future . . ." Then in one swift blow, she smashed the bottle on the ship's bow. ". . . I christen this ship *Marcellina's Mystique.*"

"May Neptune, mighty king of the sea, favor us with his blessing today!" Diego called.

"Hear! Hear!" Marcellina cheered.

"May King Neptune bring fair winds and good fortune!" Diego continued.

Marcellina cried, "Hear! Hear!"

Suddenly Tango's tail dropped and his ears flattened. Something didn't feel right. A low growl rose in his throat.

Grrr-rrr . . . ruff! Grrr-ruff-ruff-ruff!

"Shush, Tango," Marcellina scolded.

Toasting his shipmates, Diego boldly concluded: "May King Neptune nurture and care for us through perilous seas!"

CHAPTER 4

Shipwrecked

Alas, after days of good sailing on fair seas in the North Atlantic, the fickle King Neptune sent our sailors a midnight storm with perilous waves, mighty foul winds, and extremely bad fortune. Fighting giant sea swells, *Marcellina's Mystique* lost its way in the Gulf of St. Lawrence as it approached the south shore of Prince Edward Island.

There, in the first light of dawn, in the village of Victoria-by-the-Sea, a handful of people huddled around a white-haired man in a wheat-colored robe. The man wore a wooden cross around his neck and a rope belt tight around his waist.

On that first day of May, the air on the island was cool and moist. Pastor MacDougal shivered, eager to begin his Blessing of the Boats on the opening day of lobster fishing season.

Lobstermen—anxious to load dozens of lobster traps into the big bellies of their boats—scurried back and forth across the planks of the wharf to brightly painted fishing sheds on the shore.

Just a few hours earlier, a violent thunderstorm had cleansed the white wooden crafts tied to the wharf, but now the waters in Victoria Bay were steel gray and still.

Outside the villagers' circle, a tall, slender girl stirred the sand with her boot. Nearby, in a thicket of wild rose bushes, an elderly fox watched her every move.

Pastor MacDougal raised his arms and began his blessing.

The fishermen paused in their places, but did not gather.

"May God bless you and keep you," invoked Pastor MacDougal.

"Amen," Augusta Smith, a fisherman's widow, whispered.

"May God bless your boats," the pastor continued, his voice lofting like a gull soaring on the breeze.

The somber villagers nodded in unison.

"May God bless your labors and bring you safely—"

Suddenly, a high-pitched voice pierced the tail end of Pastor MacDougal's benediction.

"By George! There's a rat in that trap!"

Little Art Cody wiggled his finger at a lobster trap underneath the wharf.

His brother, Big Bart Cody, walked bow-legged in his rubber boots to Little Art's side. "There's a rat in a trap?"

The two brothers hopped off the pier and onto the beach, where a corner of the trap was mired in the sand.

Indeed, the arms and legs of a small mammal were entangled in the mesh that lined the trap. The trap's weathered wood slats were split.

Big Bart squinted at the animal's rump. "That's not the tail of a rat."

"That's not the tail of a rat?" asked his brother.

Augusta Smith, five feet ten in her stocking feet, pushed her way through the crowd, wedged her ample frame between Big Bart and Little Art, and dropped to her knees in front of the trap.

With a grunt, Augusta tugged at the trap. A strand of rope webbing snapped, and the trap broke free.

Augusta—or Miss Gustie, as the villagers called the retired schoolteacher—examined the trapped animal. Not only was the tail too short to be a rat's, but its fur was too long and multicolored, its ears too big, and its snout too pointy.

"It's a pup," Miss Gustie declared.

"It's a pup?" Little Art echoed.

Miss Gustie, a prolific knitter, used her deft fingers to untangle the chilled, wet body from the trap's webbing. "It's a pup."

From the pier, old Ben Rafferty snapped the braces on his yellow overtrousers. "Give 'im here!" he shouted in a gruff, gravely voice. "I'll use it for bait."

Miss Gustie noticed the dog's ears twitching ever so slightly. "Not on your life, Ben Rafferty!" she roared.

Miss Gustie's knees cracked as she rose. She laid two fingers on the canine's chest and felt the weak pulsing of his heart.

"He's alive," Miss Gustie told the onlookers, who stood in reverent silence behind her.

"He's alive," Priscilla, the postmistress, repeated.

"It's a miracle!" Pastor MacDougal pronounced.

CHAPTER 5

My Name Is Tango

Rat. Bait.

Tango had tried to wiggle out of the lobster trap's webbing, but he was too weak and stiff from the cold. Icicles of hair pinched his skin. His eyelids were frozen shut, his lungs tiny punching bags without air.

Rat. Bait.

Where was he?

Was he dreaming?

He couldn't be dead. He was in too much pain.

When two warm human hands untangled his limbs, Tango opened his mouth, but no sound came out. His tongue tasted like salt and dead fish. His nose was plugged.

Suddenly, his aching body sunk into a different net: soft, warm, and woolly. Hope mixed with delirium. It was Marcellina! His beloved mistress was not lost at sea in the terrible storm—Marcellina was here, holding him in her arms.

"It's okay, pup. We're almost home," he heard a woman's voice say.

Home? He was back in Manhattan?

When the woman shifted her weight, it seemed as if Tango's body might shatter.

"Who am I kidding, the darn dog's probably dead by now anyway."

Tango's body jerked. His toenails snagged on something. A searing strand of pain traveled up his leg.

Now the woman was climbing stairs—one, two, three . . . "Oh, well," she said a little more cheerfully. "The little guy deserves a decent burial, eh?"

If Tango could have, he would have moaned—a low, slow moan so melancholy that, no matter where she was, Marcellina would hear. Marcellina would come and carry him home.

"Hmm . . . I wonder what your name was."

IS . . . My name is . . .

A door creaked. Tango smelled cinnamon and burning wood. Glowing balls of light exploded behind his eyes.

IS . . . My name is . . .

No longer able to bear the pain, Tango drifted into the dark, dreamy waters between life and death.

Inky purple jellyfish wound tentacles around his neck. He tried to speak his name, but bitter water filled his lungs. When he gagged, a school of glittery minnows, sputtering like sparks, came out of his mouth.

My name is Tango, he gurgled. *My name is Tango.*

Then everything turned black.

CHAPTER 6

Links of Silver

Twelve-year-old McKenna Skye stayed on the beach as Augusta Smith hustled up Main Street with the ratty-looking dog bundled into the folds of her sweater. McKenna watched until the gray-haired woman disappeared behind a barn red door on the water side of her green-shuttered house.

"Poor Miss Gustie. She'll be sorry." Priscilla clucked. "If that dog lives, it'll be nothing but trouble, mark my words."

Pastor MacDougal tightened his belt, turning to lead the small procession of well-wishers to the end of the wharf.

He motioned to McKenna. "You're welcome to join us, Miss . . ."

McKenna, new to the village, and known only as Big Bart Cody's niece, shook her head no. During the pastor's blessing, she'd spied a glint of silver in the sand.

Once the villagers left the beach, McKenna looked around to see if anyone was watching.

To the north, the streets were empty. In the east, the rising sun striated the heavens with strands of gold. A pair of seals, their heads as black and shiny as a fisherman's slicker, swam in unison in the tranquil waters of the bay.

McKenna kicked at the sand, exposing a chain of silver links. A bracelet, it seemed, with its clasp missing.

She paused. She had a feeling that someone was watching her.

When she looked up, a three-legged cat was perched atop an upside-down dinghy. Mostly black, the cat had white fur between his chest and chin, dotted by a tiny patch of black. Once, the cat might have been a handsome animal, but the beast seemed scarred—in more ways than one.

McKenna fingered the sand-covered links. At water's edge, where the tide was going out, she dipped the silver links into a clear pool. Still seeing no one, she slipped the bracelet into the pocket of her jeans.

Near the end of the wharf, engines rumbled and diesel fumes rose in the mist. As the lobster boats pulled away, the villagers cheered, gulls cawed, and Priscilla waved a provincial flag.

McKenna ran her hand across the ridges the bracelet formed. Who would've lost it? The bracelet must've been pretty expensive . . . maybe it was her lucky day.

Talk about lucky—was the little dog still alive? She'd like to knock on the gray-haired woman's door and ask, but McKenna didn't think she would welcome the intrusion—especially from a girl she didn't know.

Anyway, it was time to get to work.

Across the street, a clapboard building stood in the corner of the Codys' backyard. The shed, Big Bart told McKenna, had originally been built—but never used—as a cure-shed for city people with tuberculosis. For the last decade or so, it had stood empty.

On the rainy night in April, a few weeks earlier, when McKenna had knocked on Big Bart's door with nothing but a sleeping bag, a backpack, and an arm full of bad bruises, Big Bart had said, "Yeah, you can stay . . ."

He offhandedly added, "Might have to sleep in the shed, though."

Big Bart Cody's frame house was already stuffed with too many children. Five, at last count, as well as his wife, named Jeannie, who was none too happy about having one more mouth to feed—especially a "niece" who Jeannie never knew existed.

Big Bart didn't ask McKenna what had driven her away from her foster home some forty miles north.

Had Big Bart asked, McKenna would've been honest: her foster father—whom McKenna called "Mr. Z."—caught her stealing a five-dollar bill from his wallet. If Big Bart had pushed further, what would McKenna have said? That she was tired of living with strangers? Tired of being tossed around?

McKenna shrugged. She ground the toe of her black boot into the sand. That's the way it was with her—always had been—trouble at school, trouble at home, as constant as the tides.

Now safe under Big Bart's wing in Victoria-by-the-Sea, the idea of having her own place—even a run-down shed—stuck in McKenna's mind. She didn't give Big Bart any peace until he agreed to let her fix the place up and, at least for the summer, sleep out there.

Yesterday, McKenna had painted the boards on the east side of the shed sea green. Today, given the promise of sunshine in the eastern sky, maybe she could finish painting another side.

CHAPTER 7

Stumped

From his post atop an upside-down dinghy, a three-legged cat named Nigel Stump observed the morning's goings-on. He was beside himself . . .

A dog that looked like a rat! *Pfff!*

In a lobster trap? *Pfff!*

A half-dead stranger taken in by a villager? *Pfff!*

Nigel recalled what it was like last winter when he hobbled into Victoria looking for food and shelter. No one gave him as much as an empty tuna can to lick.

Nigel stared at the raven-haired girl on the beach. What was *she* doing on *his* beach, staring at the sand?

Matters such as these were of grave concern to Nigel, as well they should be. He was night watchman and chief scavenger for the pack of cats that ruled the wharf. The minute he'd wandered into their territory, Nigel heard that the wharf cats were a bunch of garbage-eating, bone-splitting, nest-robbing varmints despised by every self-respecting animal in the village.

But what choice did a crippled cat from the country have? At least he had a roof over his head.

Nigel watched the girl pluck something shiny out of the sand—a keeper, it seemed. *Rats, rats, double-rats,* he thought as the girl slipped whatever it was into the pocket of her jeans.

Once the coast was clear, Nigel jumped off the dinghy.

Whiskers twitching, he circled the lobster trap.

The cat pack didn't take kindly to strange animals—especially dogs—invading their territory. Victoria-by-the-Sea was a village where everyone knew their place; the cats meant to keep it that way.

Nigel warmed at the thought of meeting up with the little dog—if it wasn't dead by now—on some dark and stormy night. He'd show the rat-boy who ruled.

Then he remembered his missing leg, severed by the teeth of a steel trap in Ben Rafferty's woods. Nigel corrected himself: *We'll* show him who ruled.

Nigel sniffed the girl's footprints. He wrinkled his nose. The soles of her boots left a pungent odor.

An outsider—and a female at that—beat him to a treasure. Just his luck . . .

Disheartened, Nigel scratched at the sand and squatted.

Suddenly, he glimpsed a slim rim of silver.

He pounced.

He scored!

Using his paw, he brushed grains of sand off the object's shiny surface.

Hmm . . . a charm . . . a heart-shaped charm. . . . The silver heart had a row of big letters on one side and three rows of letters and numbers on the other.

Nigel purred with glee. Humans *hated* losing anything with letters or numbers.

Overhead, a squad of screeching seagulls soared. Feeling uneasy, Nigel glanced around. Crouched in a cover of wild rose bushes was a bone-thin, dull-coated red fox—an outsider who'd appeared in Victoria-by-the-Sea on the very same day as the black-haired girl.

Nigel spat. What was this village coming to?

The fox emerged from the bushes with his yellow eyes fixed on Nigel. Then he bared his teeth and hissed.

That was enough for Nigel. The fox looked old, mean, and ready to go down fighting.

Nigel picked up the charm in his teeth and fled to safety.

CHAPTER 8

Warming Up

Still cradling the wet dog in her left arm, Augusta Smith opened the door of her cast-iron stove. She placed a log on top of the red coals and adjusted the flue. She moved the steaming tea kettle off the cook lid so the water would stay hot but not boil. With her right fist, she punched down the sweet dough for its second rising.

Were these small tasks so necessary, you ask, at the very moment when the little dog was teetering between life and death? Was Augusta stalling—afraid to face the fact that the dog in her arms might be dead?

One cautious step at a time, Augusta climbed the wooden staircase to the second-floor bathroom, where she pulled a fraying towel off the bar.

How foolish she'd been to hurry home, jostling the pup's body as she had. But Ben Rafferty was a mean old cuss, the kind of man who just might have used the little dog for bait!

"No, you did the right thing," Augusta assured herself.

She spread the towel over the calico quilt on her four-poster bed. Unrolling the folds of her sweater, she eased the limp dog's body onto the towel.

Augusta laid her hands on his sand-crusted fur. His body was warmer than when she'd first touched him. A gash—raw, but not bleeding—slashed his left thigh. Welts formed an imperfect ring around his neck.

"Please let the little guy live," she prayed aloud.

Gently patting the dog dry, Augusta contemplated some kind of bargain.

Lord, if you let him live, I promise I'll . . .

Promise what? What was a fair exchange?

Augusta got down on her knees. She touched the pup's button-size nose—it was dry—and, with her fingernail, brushed particles of sand out of his nostrils.

Was air moving in and out, or not? She couldn't tell. Oh, and his body seemed so terribly, terribly lifeless. Augusta's heart sank like an anchor heaved into the sea. Could she even dig a grave? It'd been a cold spring . . . was the ground soft enough?

Augusta shuddered. I won't think about it, she

decided. "Hang on there, little fellow. I'll be right back."

On the way to get a hot water bottle, Augusta stopped in front of her pine hope chest. Reverently, she lifted up a finely woven, crib-size blanket.

Had it really been over thirty years? Had it been that long since her dear Albert had drowned while laying lobster traps in a freak storm—like the one last night?

The blanket had been woven so that someday Augusta might wrap a baby of her own in it. But that day had never come.

Augusta pressed the baby blanket to her face. Her shoulders slumped.

No baby girl. No baby boy. And now?

Now, a dying dog.

Holding her breath, Augusta wrapped the injured animal in the blanket and laid the bundle next to the hot water bottle.

How had the little dog survived a beating by such a cruel sea? From where had he come? To whom did he belong?

It had been a long time since she'd felt so utterly helpless, so totally useless.

"I don't know what else to do," she said sadly. "So if it's all the same to you, little dog, I think I'll have my tea."

CHAPTER 9

Stitched Back Together

Tango swam in a sea of stormy nightmares, thrashing his legs, desperately trying to stay afloat in swirling waters. Suddenly, a school of jellyfish formed a squishy raft beneath his flailing body. Caged by wavy tentacles, his weak limbs stuck in iridescent pools of goo.

Inside the folds of a soft blanket, Tango awoke in a cold sweat. Where was he? Not a single picture formed in his mind.

Tango opened his eyes, but his sliver of sight was clouded. His snout was being stroked—by someone who smelled woolly, like the sheep on Mr. Bailey's farm.

A door creaked. "Gustie?" a man's voice called. "Gustie, are you up there?"

"We are," a woman answered.

It was not Marcellina. This woman's voice was

deep and low. Marcellina's voice was high and sweet, like the sound of a piccolo.

"It's Jack. Jack Tucker."

Jack? Gustie? Who *were* these people?

"Better than another hot dish," the woman named Gustie called back as the footsteps grew closer.

Little did Tango know that his miraculous rescue was the biggest news in the village since Priscilla's grandfather had celebrated his one hundredth birthday. For hours, a parade of well-wishers had been dropping by Augusta's house with food: corn relish, clam chowder, strawberry-rhubarb pie, raspberry-rhubarb pie, blueberry-rhubarb pie, baking powder biscuits, a bag of mussels, live lobsters packed on ice.

"I'm beginning to feel like the guest of honor at my own funeral."

The man named Jack laughed. "So, where's the lucky rat—I mean, dog—that I've heard so much about?"

"He's right here."

Lucky? Rat?

Tango was so confused. His head was pounding, as if someone wearing spike heels were stepping on his skull, pressing his eyelids shut, forcing him back into darkness.

∞

When he opened his eyes, Tango thought that he'd been asleep for days. In fact, it had been only a few minutes. In the dim room, the murky outline of a tall man loomed over him.

Diego! It must be Diego!

He's here with Marcellina. They've come to take me home!

Tango sniffed. No . . . it wasn't Diego. He sniffed again. This man's hands smelled like medicine and sheep manure.

Now Tango's blanketed body was being unwrapped. Something cold pressed against his throbbing chest.

"Hmm . . . weak, irregular . . ."

The man checked Tango's ears and peeled back his eyelids. A pull. A pinch. A blinding beam of light.

When the man's fingernails grazed the wound on Tango's left side, Tango made his first sound, a meager whine, like a kitten mewing.

The man lifted Tango's right hind leg and stretched his left.

Stop. Please. You're killing me, Tango groaned in a language that humans could not understand.

The man tugged on Tango's paws. "I've eaten chicken wings with more meat on the bones than these."

"This is no time for sarcasm, Jack."

Those voices. Now Tango remembered: the woolly woman who'd untangled him from the trap. And Jack—the man who called him a lucky rat.

"What's this, Gustie?" asked Jack.

"What's what? And for heaven's sake, call me Augusta. We're not children anymore."

"Looks like he's bleeding."

Tango cringed.

"Oh my."

"He's in rough shape, Augusta. I don't think he's going to make it."

"I'll thank you to keep your opinions to yourself, Jack Tucker."

"I'm a vet. People pay for my opinions." Jack sighed. "I just don't want you to get your hopes up."

A vet? Tango was in an animal hospital?

Tango heard human hands rubbing together, a soft scratching of skin on skin.

"Just tell me what needs to be done," said Augusta curtly.

"Right now, the dog needs stitches, antibiotics, and, to be on the safe side, a tetanus shot."

A window shade rolled, giving light to the room.

"But you'll have to hold him down."

Oh, no! A SHOT!

"Poor pup."

"Oh, he's not a pup," said Jack. "He's full grown—

some kind of terrier, I think. He's so beat up, it's hard to tell, eh?"

The woman's hands held Tango's body firmly but gently. A steel needle drove deep into Tango's rump.

Just let me die, Tango pleaded. *Just let me die.*

Finally, the needle eased out, leaving a burning tingle. Tango felt dizzy—a sleepy, spinning out of control.

"A Yorkshire Terrier, probably," Jack said. "You know, in all my years of practice, I don't think I've ever seen one on the island."

What island?

Tango tried to untangle his thoughts, but as the veterinarian started stitching, he slipped back into the sea.

CHAPTER 10

The Pitiful Place

The now-deserted home of Old Ada Phillips was built on the rocky shore just west of the wharf in Victoria-by-the-Sea. Villagers, Nigel Stump knew, called the dilapidated structure the Pitiful Place.

Indeed its peeling blue paint did appear to be weeping. The windows were shaded and sad. A bare, warped board above the door resembled a frown.

With the thin silver heart clenched in his teeth, Nigel scrambled up a wooden ramp that led to a one-hinged door. He squeezed through a space between the door and its frame, pausing to inhale the deliciously pervasive ratty smell.

Even into her mideighties, Old Ada had rescued white mice and rats discarded by biomedical laboratories. After the good-hearted but eccentric woman died, village councilmen filled burlap sacks with a few heavy rocks and—what they believed was—

every last one of the rodents. Mice, rats, and rocks were tossed into the sea.

Nigel found the other cats—Axel, Tate, Leftie, Flint, and Briar—lounging about in the main room. Amid stacks of decades-old newspapers, trash, bones, broken lamps, and bird skulls were dozens of empty rodent cages, both steel and glass.

On his very first scavenger hunt, Nigel found a set of car keys that he'd hung on one of the cages. He'd been scavenging and decorating ever since, trying to make the place feel like a real home.

Axel, a brown-striped tabby with a sharp tongue, was the cats' self-appointed leader. His former owner had chopped off the tip of Axel's tail with—you guessed it—an ax, a brutal act which Axel vowed never to forget.

Axel insisted that Nigel adopt the name Stump to prove that he, too, had renounced the domesticated life.

In Nigel's heart and mind, Nigel was still Nigel.

Tate, Leftie, Flint, and Briar had their own tales of maltreatment. It was part of the glue that held the gang of cats together.

Nigel drooled in anticipation of the envy the silver charm would evoke. He leaped from the back of a wing chair to the fireplace mantle—no easy feat for a three-legged cat.

"What's up, Stump?" asked Axel.

Nigel revealed the heart-shaped piece of silver that crowned the tip of his tongue.

"For me?" asked the blue-furred female named Briar.

Tate, a black cat with an even darker spirit, eyed the charm and, with a casual flick of his seriously long tail, dismissed its value.

"Way to go, Stump," said Leftie, who'd lost his right ear to a Pit Bull Terrier. "Where'd ya find it?"

Nigel let the heart drop onto a cracked saucer. "On the beach. Washed up in the storm, I guess."

"That was a whopper of a storm," Leftie commented, pointing his orange paw at a puddle of water by the refrigerator, which lay like a white coffin in the middle of the room.

Somehow, the discovery of the shiny charm had empowered Nigel. Something had been eating away at him for weeks. It was time to speak up.

"Hey, guys . . ."

Not a single eye turned in Nigel's direction.

"Guys?"

"Say what ya gotta say," Tate hissed. Nigel glared at the cats until he had their complete attention.

"*We* have a problem," he announced. "The *village* has a problem. For all I know, the whole *island* has a problem."

Grins broke out all around. The cat pack loved

problems, troubles, sorrows, and other states of anxiety and fear.

Briar stopped grooming her luscious blue fur. "What's the problem, Stumpy?"

"Outsiders." Nigel curled the word off his tongue with disgust. "They're invading our village."

"Stump, what're you talking about?" demanded Axel.

"As you know—today is the opening day of lobster season," Nigel continued.

More grins. The cats loved lobster season—all the succulent scraps that littered the wharf after the fishermen unloaded their traps.

"Just a little while ago, at the wharf," explained Nigel, "one of the men saw—I mean, he thought he saw—a rat tangled in a lobster trap." He puffed out his chest. "Fresh meat."

Briar smacked her lips. "I *love* rat steak."

"But it turns out, it was a dog. A very small dog."

"A dog in a lobster trap?" Axel sneered. "You gotta be kidding. Where'd it come from?"

"My point exactly," said Nigel. "Where are all of these foreigners coming from? And why?"

"Who else," asked Briar, "besides the dog?"

"That girl—the one with long black hair. She's strange, I tell you—always hanging around our beach, stealing our stuff."

"No stranger than any of the other two-leggers in the village," Leftie noted. "Who else?"

"The fox," Nigel snarled. "That foul creature showed up on the same day as the girl. No coincidence, if you ask me."

"Strange. Very strange indeed," agreed Tate.

"A strange girl, a fox, and now this Rat-Boy," Nigel complained.

Flint, a Siamese Cross, yawned. "Who's Rat-Boy?"

Fur on end, Nigel bared his brownish teeth. "Flint, listen up! Rat-Boy's the name I gave the new dog! We've got to call him something."

With narrowed eyes, Axel stroked his whiskers with a paw. "Three outsiders moving into the village since the snow melted. If this keeps up, by next spring, that's—"

"Too many," Briar declared.

"This calls for a plan," concluded Axel, switching his tipless tail.

An odd smile skewed the tabby cat's face—a sinister look that Nigel hadn't seen before.

"The Scram Plan." Axel sniggered. "Effective immediately."

CHAPTER 11

Kindred Spirits

Nigel was correct. It was no coincidence that Beau Fox showed up in Victoria-by-the-Sea on the same day as McKenna Skye. So, while we give our little friend Tango some time to heal, we'll meander back in time—twelve years or so, to another shore.

The unlikely bond between the girl and the fox formed during the second summer of Beau's life.

A few hours before dawn, Beau was curled inside his den, deep in the sand dunes on the North Shore. Above him, meadow mice tittered and skittered, reminding Beau of his hunger. He unfurled his tail, stretched, and stuck his head out of the den. A thin wail, carried on the northeast wind, cut through the familiar buzzing, humming, lapping, and flapping sounds of the night.

Beau's black ears perked. He sniffed the air. The sound unsettled him. With his hind paws stepping into tracks left by his front paws, he trotted across the sand in search of its source.

As he approached the marsh near North River, the cry became thicker, more desperate. The fur on Beau's back bristled. This was not the final cry of a frog clasped in the jaws of a raccoon. Not a rabbit's squeal, nor a plea for mercy from a mole clamped in an owl's beak.

Heavy spring rains had caused the river to over-flow its banks. Crabs scattered as Beau plodded through the slimy marsh grasses. He found himself sinking in muck and once had to swim to safety.

The wail peaked, broke, and rose again to a screech.

Winds blew the clouds off the face of a full moon, exposing a brilliant white path of light across the marsh. Just ahead, a solid dark bundle was wedged between the trunks of two silver birches. Four tiny flesh-covered limbs rose out of the dark mass, kick-ing and thrashing.

Cautiously, Beau approached. A step. Another step.

And then—a baby. A human baby. Very small. Very young.

Beau held a point, prepared to pounce.

The dark-haired infant screamed. Beau retreated. Water swirled close to the white hairs at the bottom of his chest.

When the infant's voice stilled, Beau moved forward and sniffed. The terrified baby's glassy eyes widened. Tears streamed down the plump flesh of its cheeks. Beau growled. For a moment, he considered biting the soft flesh. Such sweet revenge it would be.

Beau's mind flashed back to a sleeting night in late winter. The distant squeal of tires. The scream of his mate, Tawny—her body crushed by the tires of a bright red car. When Beau reached her, it was too late.

Shaking off his grief, Beau studied his discovery.

The infant, he realized, was lying in a basket woven out of reeds and green branches. It was lined with the feathered skin of a goose. All but one of the leather cords binding the baby to its makeshift cradle had loosened.

Finally, the baby's cries of desperation cut deep into Beau's heart, cracking a frozen spot. Beau touched his nose to the infant's wet forehead. He licked its salty cheek, and the crying ceased. The infant squirmed; innocent arms reached out to him.

Suddenly, a powerful eddy dislodged the cradle.

Beau lunged and caught the infant's foot in his mouth. The infant screamed. Beau softened his grip but did not let go.

Stepping backward, Beau tried to pull the cradled infant to safety. But as soon as he gained a little ground, the water propelled him backward. Finally, using one last burst of strength, Beau pulled the baby and its water-logged basket out of the swirling water to a bed of needles under a fir tree.

Beau smelled blood. The infant's foot was bleeding. Beau saw that it was a girl-child. Beau was weak with exhaustion, sick with fear that the baby's scent would be picked up by a predator. Beau had the will to tow the infant to the safety of his den—but not the strength.

He curled his bushy tail around her body and licked her wounded foot. The infant quieted, and they slept.

A few hours later, screams of hunger pierced the predawn air.

Beau opened his eyes, for a moment confused. Two Great Blue heron towered above them. The baby—perhaps out of fear—stopped crying.

"You can't keep her," the male—whom Beau now recognized as the bird called King—pronounced.

"She's human! She can't survive," said the female, known as Queen.

"You must return her to her own kind," warned King, "before it's too late."

Beau brushed his snout across wisps of black hair on the baby's head. "Do you know what happened?"

"No. But sometimes humans give up their young to the water." King glanced at the soggy scraps of feathered goose skin still tied to the baby. "Whatever happened, it happened in the Old Way."

"The Old Way?" questioned Beau.

"At birth," explained Queen, "babies of the First Nation were dipped into the coldest water that could be found and—"

An owl perched on a nearby pine branch completed Queen's sentence. "They were wrapped in warm furs and sometimes—in the skin of a wild goose."

King pointed his thin, sharp beak at Beau. "Her fate is for humans to decide. Intervention is noble but unwise."

The infant's whimpers tore at Beau's heart.

"The closest human house is—"

"I know where it is," Beau said forlornly.

It was the house with the killing machine parked in front of it—the red car that had taken Tawny. Beau felt overwhelmed; the responsibility was too great.

"Fox! Now! You must act," King commanded. "Take her there, or she will die."

"Dig roots for her to suck on—to keep her quiet," Queen instructed.

"I saw a large piece of net lying on the beach," said Owl.

"Show me," said King. "But hurry. Dawn is coming."

∞

Led by Owl, Beau and the heron dragged the netted infant along a moss-covered trail near the shoreline. The trio came as close to the two-story house as they dared, stopping outside a circle of mowed grass.

Plopping drops of rain now fell on the baby's face. The root dropped out of her mouth, and she began to cry.

King, Queen, and Owl flew off, but Beau backed into the bushes.

In the house, a light came on. The front door opened. A slight, blond woman stood in the door-way. When she saw the baby, the woman brought her hands to her face, and then dashed to where the naked infant lay.

His heart full of sadness—foreign, yet familiar—Beau returned to his den. But he couldn't get the baby out of his mind. And so, at sunrise the next morning, he returned to the human's house, where he dug a burrow in the base of a huge woodpile.

∞

The girl, who was named McKenna Skye, would move often. But wherever McKenna went—no

matter how many different adults she lived with—
Beau followed, bound by a loyalty he neither understood nor questioned.

Wherever McKenna was, that was home. Kindred
spirits are like that.

For twelve years, Beau was the girl's ever-
present shadow. Beau kept his distance, never sure
if McKenna realized the strength of their bond, or
the depth of his love.

And then, on another night when the moon was
golden and full, McKenna Skye yelled into the shadows, "Hey, fox! I'm leaving! For good! Are you coming or not?"

And, once again, Beau followed.

CHAPTER 12

Missing Identity

One afternoon, about a week after he washed ashore, Tango lay sleeping on a pastel blanket that lined a crate next to the rocking chair where Augusta knitted.

The *creak-creak-creak* of the rockers kept time with the *click-click-click* of Augusta's needles. The *coo-coo* of the tiny bird that lived inside Augusta's wooden clock reminded Tango how slowly the hours were passing. Whenever he opened his eyes, it seemed to be raining.

He didn't know where he was, except that he was on an island, he'd overheard Augusta say. *An island? Like Manhattan?* Tango wondered.

Tango recalled little of that thick-clouded, rain-thrashed night when a giant wave swept him off Diego's sailboat into the sea. What he did recall made his teeth chatter and his limbs shake.

Now when he heard Augusta say, "All he does is sleep," Tango stirred.

The man, the veterinarian Jack Tucker, was smiling down on him. "How's his appetite?"

"Getting better," answered Augusta.

At first, Tango had licked drops of water off Augusta's fingers. Then she fed him sips of broth from an eye dropper and, after that, a beef-flavored paste on a tiny silver spoon. Earlier that day, Augusta had given him bits of chicken.

"It's time to check the little guy's stitches. How are they holding up?"

"How am I holding up is the question," Augusta replied. "I may have bitten off more than I can chew. Taking care of an injured dog is a full-time job."

Jack pulled back the corner of Tango's stained, foul-smelling blanket.

"I should've washed it, but when I try, he holds it in his teeth and growls."

Jack lifted Tango and his blanket and laid the bundle on Augusta's bed.

Tango moaned.

"Sorry, little buddy."

With gentle fingers, Jack pressed Tango's muscles and bones, gauging Tango's reaction. Tango winced, but didn't squeal.

"So, what are you going to name him?" asked Jack.

"Why, I'm not," said Augusta.

"The dog has to have a name."

She can't name me! I have a name.

"Well, I'm not going to," said Augusta curtly. "Soon as I do, somebody or other will show up in Victoria looking for their dog—and then what?"

A ray of hope poked Tango's heart. Augusta believed that Marcellina would come looking for him. Soon! Maybe even today! Tango imagined his glowing, appreciative mistress showering Augusta with fistfuls of green dollars—and how the two of them would drive off in a stretch limousine.

Jack pointed at the sheets of newspaper spread under Tango's makeshift bed. "Have you checked the lost-and-found ads?"

"Um, yes, I intend to, but . . ."

"I can save you the trouble," Jack interrupted. "The only lost dog on the whole island is a black lab."

Tango's brief bubble of hope burst.

"So, what *are* you going to name him?"

Anger rippled across Tango's tender skin.

I have a name! My name is Tango! It's right on my name tag . . .

Suddenly it hit him: his silver heart, his silver collar—they were gone!

If Augusta had Tango's identification tag, Tango realized, she'd know his name. She'd know that he belonged to Marcellina LaTour, who lived in Manhattan.

Where could his heart and collar be?

Dejected, Tango answered his own question: at the bottom of the sea.

He buried his snout between his paws, feeling stranded, lonely, and forgotten.

Augusta folded her arms across her chest. "Even if no one comes around asking for him, who's to say I'll even keep him? He'd be a nuisance to have around the shop."

What kind of shop would he be a nuisance around? Tango liked shops. Besides, Marcellina never once accused him of being a nuisance, and they went shopping all the time—nearly every day.

"Here, I've got something to show you." Jack placed a glossy piece of paper in Augusta's hand. "See. I was right. He's a Yorkshire Terrier."

Tango wished he could see the picture.

"But this dog doesn't have long hair like *that*," she said. "His hair is short."

"Probably means that he wasn't a show dog," Jack said. "This is how some folks fix these critters up. Ribbons, bows, perfume—the works."

"Well, even if I were to keep him, I certainly wouldn't let him run around the village looking like an old mop. Why, it'd be bad for business."

Jack Tucker laughed. "You could call him Mopsy—you know, Flopsy, Mopsy, Cottontail, and . . ."

"Nope—I'm not ready," said Augusta. " 'Pup' will do for now."

Pup? Tango groaned. *She can't call me Pup!* Pup was such a silly, insignificant name.

Once, he remembered, he'd felt the same way about the name Tango.

Tango. Like the dance.

Tango burrowed his face in the pastel blanket and breathed in the smell of his own sickness. His misery simmered. If this is the way it was, Tango didn't want to go on living.

Feed him to the fish! He didn't care.

CHAPTER 13

Lost and Found

The southeast corner of Augusta Smith's backyard met the northwest corner of Big Bart Cody's property. Augusta's yard was square, bound by a white picket fence, and bordered with tulips, daffodils, and lilacs anxious to bloom. An ancient oak tree, tall and regal, with deep roots, stood in the center.

On a good drying day, sunny, with a crisp wind cutting across Victoria Bay, McKenna heard the *flap-snap-crack* of bed sheets on Miss Gustie's clothesline. She balanced her brush on the rim of a can of butter yellow paint, stood up, and stretched.

Painting the trim on her shed was a lot harder, she realized, than rolling sea green paint up and down its walls.

A petite face—not unlike that of a fox cub—was framed between the pickets of Miss Gustie's fence. The furry face had a black nose and two dark eyes not much bigger than buttons. It must be the little dog Miss Gustie had rescued at the beach a couple of weeks ago.

McKenna was surprised to see the dog outside. She'd heard that he was taking a long time to heal. Doc Tucker was over to Miss Gustie's place so often, people were beginning to talk about a romance between them.

McKenna felt sorry for the little guy—away from home, taken in by a stranger.

A few feet from the dog, McKenna crouched low to the ground, urging him to sniff her fingers. From over the fence, she heard a gruff voice.

"Why aren't you in school, young lady?"

The little dog disappeared. Miss Gustie's hands appeared on the pointed ends of the pickets.

"I don't have to go to school if I don't want to," McKenna answered. "And . . . I don't want to."

Miss Gustie gave McKenna the once-over, from the tips of her boots to the part in the center of her hair. "How old are you, if I may ask?"

McKenna dropped her chin. "Um . . . uh . . . almost sixteen."

"No, you're twelve, thirteen at most," observed the grizzly haired woman. "You belong in school."

McKenna didn't argue. Miss Gustie, she'd heard, used to be a teacher, and teachers, well—they always thought they knew what was best for you.

"What's Bart Cody thinking, harboring a truant, for heaven's sake?" Miss Gustie pursed her lips. "He ought to know better . . ."

The wind picked up. The sheets somersaulted over Miss Gustie's clothesline with a *smack!*

"Well, what do you have to say for yourself?"

"Uncle Bart says the school year's almost over. He figures that once the lobstermen take to the boats, teachers don't teach much anyways. He said I'll learn plenty, fixing up the shed."

Miss Gustie rolled her eyes. "That may be the case where the Codys are from, but not around here."

"Anyways, I've got work to do. Tourists will be showing up any day now. I've got to get my stuff ready."

Miss Gustie's tone of voice changed: more curious than scolding. "Stuff? What kind of stuff?" She extended her hand. "Oh, by the way, I'm Augusta Smith. We've not been introduced."

"I know who you are." McKenna meant to shake Miss Gustie's hand, but stopped when she realized that her fingers were spotted with wet paint.

"And you are . . . I mean, besides being Big Bart's niece?"

"McKenna. McKenna Skye." She scanned Miss Gustie's yard, wondering where the little dog went. "So, what did you name your dog?"

"I haven't."

"You haven't?"

"He's not my dog," answered Miss Gustie emphatically. "I call him Pup. Good enough for now—until his people come for him."

His people weren't going to come for him, McKenna thought. No more than her real mother ever came back for her.

With his nose to the ground, the little dog was zigzagging toward the back door.

"Doesn't care to be outside, much less relieve himself out here," Miss Gustie made clear. "Clings to an old blanket I wrapped him in the first day. Half the time, he seems scared out of his skin."

"Can I see him? Up close, I mean."

"Why, um, certainly. . . ."

Miss Gustie lifted the latch and opened the gate. The dog was pressing his front paws against the back door. Miss Gustie picked him up and carried him back to where McKenna was standing.

Since the first day of lobster fishing season, McKenna had been checking the "Lost and Found" section in *The Charlottetown Guardian*. If Miss Gustie really wanted the little dog's people to come, why hadn't she placed an ad?

Miss Gustie lightly ran her finger over the stitches on his thigh. "He's pretty banged up."

"Looks like he needs a bath." McKenna stroked

the dog's snout with a clean finger. "But he sure is cute. His people must be pretty upset, losing a nice little dog like this."

"I suppose you're right."

"If he were mine, I'd be checking the lost-and-found ads every day."

Miss Gustie flinched. Her face reddened. "Why, yes, indeed."

Miss Gustie glanced at McKenna's shed. "And, uh, well—I don't mean to pry, mind you—but why are you fixing up that old shed?"

"I was thinking I might set up a little shop," McKenna said.

"And what do you plan to sell?"

"Candles," McKenna blurted, surprised by how easily her secret spilled out.

"Candles? What kind of candles?"

"Come on, I'll show you."

Propped against the trunk of a weeping willow was a piece of wood. The board's irregular shape was not unlike the shape of Prince Edward Island— the way, on a map, the island looked like a cradle rocking in the sea.

The butter yellow paint was already dry. Allowing a little pride to sneak into her voice, McKenna explained, "I need to paint inside the grooves. The letters will be rose-colored, easier to see."

"Enchanted candles?" Miss Gustie's eyes narrowed. "*Magic* candles? Is that what you mean?"

McKenna shrugged her shoulders. She didn't know if the candles were magic or not, but she meant to find out. If they were, she'd make a fortune!

"I like the way 'enchanted candles' sounds."

Miss Gustie raised her eyebrow. "I certainly hope you aren't into that voodoo-vampire stuff I read about in the papers nowadays. People in the village won't tolerate that type of foolishness."

"Uncle Bart said I could stay the summer if I could pay my own way. Candles can't be that hard to make."

"Enchanted candles," repeated Miss Gustie skeptically.

Nestled in Miss Gustie's arms, the dog whimpered. Short black whiskers sprouted from the caramel-colored hair on his cheeks.

If he were my dog, McKenna thought, I'd name him Rusty, or Whiskers.

"If you don't mind me asking, Miss Skye—do you have other family here on the island?" Miss Gustie rubbed her chin. "I don't believe I've heard the name Skye before."

McKenna took a deep breath, recalling that day in February when her social worker, Mrs. Gaspé, got careless with McKenna's case file.

McKenna had opened the manila folder and read the report—the report that said that McKenna's birth mother had abandoned her when she was an infant. That the woman who McKenna thought was her real mother—Pamela Skye—was killed in an auto accident when she was two.

Miss Gustie interrupted McKenna's troubled thoughts. "I understand that you're from up around Lennox Island."

"Maybe."

"Well, are you, or aren't you?"

"I'm—I—"

McKenna didn't know where she was from. Or whom she belonged to.

Miss Gustie's eyes softened as she scratched behind Pup's ears. Miss Gustie had eyes like Annie Pike—the only foster mother McKenna had ever loved.

She'd better be careful. If not, she might spill the truth.

"Where I'm from is where I am. I walk alone."

Miss Gustie seemed troubled by McKenna's remark. The creases on her forehead deepened.

"Nobody in this world walks alone." She paused. "And if they do, they don't like it. Sometimes, McKenna, it means they don't like themselves."

Did she like herself? What difference did it make?

"Well, I've got to get back to work," McKenna said.

The dog had buried his sweet face into the folds of Miss Gustie's heather blue sweater.

"Nice dog," murmured McKenna wistfully. "A person could get real attached to a nice little dog like that."

CHAPTER 14

A Festering Wound

One afternoon, in spite of the soothing sunshine, Nigel Stump was in particularly low spirits. Parked on a sandstone rock, he was trying to figure out why he didn't feel like hanging out with the cat pack.

Ever since he'd scored the silver charm, the cats had been acting strange, especially Briar and Flint.

The pack had planned to eat some newborn chicks they'd picked off in a nearby coop. When Nigel announced that he wasn't hungry, and he was going to the beach, Flint said in a syrupy tone of voice, "Stumpy-Boy, if you see that mean old outsider fox, you tell him to scram now, you hear?"

Nigel should've been elated. They'd listened to Nigel's concerns, hadn't they? Axel had announced the Scram Plan, hadn't he?

Nigel jumped off the rock. Unsteadily, he paced back and forth across the sand.

Was Nigel only imagining their disdain? He had to know.

Nigel crept back to the Pitiful Place. He peered through a hole that another animal—most likely a rat—had chewed in the boards on the wharf side.

Inside, the five cats circled a pile of yellow-feathered carcasses, as if warming themselves by a slow-burning fire.

"That Stump! What a hoot!" Flint spit out a mouthful of feathers. "I can't get over it!"

With an ugly chuckle, Leftie mimicked Nigel. "Skunks are invading our village! Skunks are invading our shores!"

"We have a problem!"

"The village of Victoria has a problem!"

"The whole of Prince Edward Island has a problem!"

Nigel cringed at the mocking chorus of laughter.

"And what's with the big words?" asked Flint. "Stump thinks he's smarter than the rest of us. It's starting to get on my nerves."

"Cut him a break, would ya? The guy's a cripple," said Axel.

"Axel, fess up," Leftie challenged. "You felt sorry for him. That's why you took him in."

"Maybe," Axel conceded. "But Stump's a good night watchman. Any of you want the job? If so, I'll get rid of him."

"I know I feel a lot better now that we've got the Scram Plan," said Tate sarcastically.

"Yeah, me, too," Briar sneered.

The cats' laughter felt like raw wind whipping across Nigel's ears.

Until today, Nigel thought that he'd never been more miserable than when Ben Rafferty's trap snapped shut on his left front paw. Nigel could still hear the sound of steel meeting steel, crunching, crushing his bones. In order to escape, he'd had to chew off his leg; if he hadn't, Nigel probably would've died right there in the trap.

Three-legged but free, Nigel laid low, licking his ragged wound. Once it healed, he was too ashamed to go back to his mother and their human family. So when Axel invited Nigel to hole up with the cats, Nigel felt like a big man. Nigel had been an only kitten. He sensed a brotherhood, a camaraderie unlike anything he'd ever known.

Now, at this moment, perhaps another cat—a cat with more self-respect—would have walked away. But Nigel Stump was not that cat.

No, he'd learned his lesson. From now on, he'd keep his mouth shut and do what he was told.

Acting as if he didn't have a care in the world, Nigel slipped back into the Pitiful Place. Out of the corner of his eye, Nigel saw Briar wink at Flint.

Nigel sprang up to the fireplace mantle. He curled

his black-and-white body around the saucer on which the silver heart was displayed. As his so-called friends licked yellow down off their paws, anxiety crawled up, down, and across Nigel's skin like a party of ants.

CHAPTER 15

The Recipe

One still evening at twilight, McKenna brought her knees to her chest. For more than an hour, she'd been trapped in the corner of her shed.

Above the silence, frogs croaked, an owl hooted, and flocks of crows chattered in the budding trees. Her stomach growled.

Earlier, she'd come in out of the steady rain, swept, and sponged down the floorboards. She'd stirred a pail of whitewash and with a big brush, hurriedly slopped on the lime solution. McKenna had started at the doorway, where the light was strongest, and worked her way backward.

Think before you act, think before you act. . . . Isn't that what her social worker was always telling her to do? If she couldn't paint a stupid floor without painting herself into a corner, how was she ever going to make it all the way to Toronto?

Maybe she should give up, phone Mrs. Gaspé—and let her come haul McKenna away to some "school" for "girls like her."

McKenna's rolled sleeping bag was hanging on the doorknob. Where was she going to sleep? No way was she walking into Jeannie Cody's kitchen with whitewashed feet to ask for a bed, or the couch.

The woman didn't like McKenna. McKenna didn't know why. Lately, at mealtimes, McKenna dished up a plate of food and ate by herself at the picnic table.

McKenna rubbed the spot between her eyebrows where her headaches always took hold. Beneath the floor, she heard the now-familiar sound of her friend, the fox, burrowing a tunnel.

Sometimes, McKenna imagined that her birth mother was dead, but had come back to this earth—not as a spirit, but as a fox. Why else would a wild animal shadow McKenna her entire life?

With a long stretch, McKenna reached for a multicolored cloth pouch, suspended from a peg under the porthole window. She dug inside for Bun-Bun, a dirty gray and tailless toy she'd carried with her for as long as she could remember.

Deep inside his stuffing, the tiny music box still worked. McKenna wound the key. She chewed the inside of her cheek and bit her lips. By the time the cradle song finished, a few tears had escaped. These she wiped away with her sleeve.

Then she dug out a black, leather-bound book with a broken binding. The pages were water-damaged; the cover curled at the corners. When she was about seven, McKenna discovered it inside a broken-down desk in Annie Pike's attic. When McKenna showed it to her foster mother, Annie didn't recognize the boy's name engraved on its cover.

"It's a Bible," Annie had said with a smile. "Finders, keepers."

Behind Annie's back, McKenna took Mr. Pike's pocketknife and scratched off the boy's gold-lettered name.

To this day, she never knew why the Pike family couldn't take her along when they moved to Toronto. But McKenna had quickly learned that foster kids don't get answers to those kinds of questions.

Fingering the Bible's scar, McKenna recalled the moment when she'd discovered a piece of paper between two pages of the Psalms.

Enchanted Candles—written in faded, delicate penmanship—was centered at the top of the parchment paper. At the bottom, a sentence was starred: *This recipe makes 13 pillar candles.*

Often, she'd searched the recipe for hidden meaning, but found none. By the time she turned twelve,

McKenna was convinced that it was her destiny to create these candles. She'd started collecting the ingredients, now in baby food jars on the shelf above her.

McKenna struck a match and traced the words on the paper, whispering the list of ingredients she'd long since memorized.

To melted paraffin, add:
One tablespoon of white sand from the North Shore
Two tablespoons of red earth from the South Shore
A strand of bark from a silver birch tree
Scrapings from the opalescence of three blue mussel
  shells
Thirteen dried purple lupine blossoms
A sprig of fireweed at peak color
One snail's shell, crushed
One sand dollar, finely ground

It was kind of spooky—it was like the *Enchanted Candles* recipe had known that she would travel from the North Shore to Victoria, on the South Shore, even before she did.

She had yet to find a sand dollar. Not that it would be easy, but finding "mermaid's money" was the least of McKenna's worries. There had to be more to making candles than melting wax, but what?

McKenna had no clue.

McKenna dug deeper into the pouch, feeling for

the silver chain she'd found on the beach. After feeling her way past a half-broken dreamcatcher, the wrinkled red envelope with Annie's address in the corner, a tube of lip balm, a pack of gum, and a wallet, she found the chain. She'd tried the bracelet on her wrist, but the chain was too long—around her neck, too short. An ankle bracelet, maybe?

McKenna took off her socks. She wound the silver links around her left ankle—perfect! With a string of leather from the dreamcatcher, she tied the two end-links together.

Later, surrounded by darkness, McKenna leaned against the wall, cradling her neck with her sweat-shirt. Hoping to fall asleep, she recited the names of months, like Annie had taught her—in the Old Way.

She began with April, when she'd run away: *Egg hatching time . . . frog croaking time . . . leaves are budding time . . . animal fur thickens time . . . ripening time . . . mate calling time. . . .*

McKenna drummed her thigh, trying to remember October, but couldn't. Hungry and frustrated, she covered her face with her hands.

Big Bart told her that whitewash dried quickly. McKenna sure hoped he was right because she had to open her shop soon. As nice as the South Shore was, she couldn't hang around Victoria-by-the-Sea forever. Just like Miss Gustie's dog, someone might come looking for *her* one of these days.

CHAPTER 16

Without Hope

One evening in late May, the sky above Prince Edward Island was deep lavender with fleeting wisps of silver clouds. In the west, the sun lingered, and then, like a strawberry red ball slipping out of a child's hand, dropped out of sight.

Tango was lying on a braided rug next to a clay pot in which a thick-stemmed geranium grew. Through a canopy of crimson petals, Augusta smiled down on him. The deep folds of skin on Augusta's face reminded Tango of a Shar-Pei that he'd once longed to meet.

"Here, Pup, I have something for you."

A tiny scarf with a teensy red pattern dangled from Augusta's fingers. The fringed scarf was woven out of dark green wool.

"See the pattern? Those are little lobsters."

Luckily, the kind doctor had just given Tango a

warm, sudsy bath. He offered Augusta a bottle of tearless shampoo. "Be sure to get him dry behind the ears," he cautioned.

Augusta cupped Tango's belly, easing him into a standing position. "Let's see how this looks."

Augusta wrapped the scarf around his neck and knotted it, not too loose and not too tight. The fringe whispered across his chest.

Tango licked Augusta's fingertips in appreciation.

❧

Sadly, no matter how kind Augusta was, as May turned to June, Tango was unable to shed his longing for the past. Love, loyalty, and regret hung on his heart like heavy ornaments hooked on the lowest branch of a Christmas tree.

A string of "if-onlys" tangled his thoughts: If only Marcellina hadn't given Diego a sailboat. If only Diego's sailboat hadn't been rocked by giant waves in a vicious sea. If only Tango hadn't lost his silver heart.

He worried, too. Had Marcellina and Diego survived the wicked storm?

One fitful night, Tango dreamed that his sister Esperanza was gazing out of a window near the top of a red and white striped lighthouse.

Tan-go . . . Tan-go . . . Esperanza called in a voice both mysterious and inviting. Keeping time with the blinking beam of light, she chanted, *Without hope . . . without hope . . . nothing is . . . nothing is. . . .*

Tango awoke with a start. His skin tingled. Esperanza was trying to tell him something. But what? He had to know!

Tango bolted to the mud room and pushed—headfirst—through the small swinging door once used, Augusta said, by her mother's cats. He scurried across Augusta's moonlit backyard, squeezed under a loose picket in the fence, and sprinted past McKenna's shed. Boldly, he headed toward the Victoria lighthouse—identical, Tango realized, to the candy cane striped structure in his dream.

Just as Tango was about to cross Water Street, a strange, scratchy voice startled him: "Where are you going?"

Tango cringed, smelling for clues.

"Yes, you, little dog."

From under the branches of a weeping willow tree emerged a skinny, doglike animal with black ears and amber eyes. In the murky light, the halo of thick fur around the animal's face echoed the eerie beauty of the moon. The animal looked familiar—yes, now Tango remembered: a red fox. Once, when he was a puppy, walking along Cold Creek, he'd seen one. A distant canine cousin, Sadie had explained. Wild—with a reputation for being cunning and sly.

Tango swallowed the lump in his throat. "Uh, um . . . who are you?"

"Beau is my name. Beau Fox," the animal said politely, peering at Tango. "And you? You are the dog named Rat-Boy."

"Rat-Boy?" snapped Tango. "My name isn't Rat-Boy!"

Beau scowled, reprimanding Tango with his eyes.

Tango dropped his tail. "My name is Tango."

"The animals in the village call you Rat-Boy—you may as well get used to it."

Tango's back hairs bristled. "Why would they call me Rat-Boy? They don't even know me."

"Don't you remember?"

"Remember what?"

"That morning on the beach—when you washed ashore. The humans thought you were a drowned rat."

"Yeah, I remember . . . sort of."

"Nigel Stump made up the name."

"Who's Nigel Stump?"

"One of those despicable felines who *think* they rule the wharf."

The fox circled Tango. Tango stiffened when the bristles on Beau's tail brushed across his back.

"And who are you—other than Tango?" Beau shook his head. "Such a strange name."

Cousin or no, could Tango trust the fox? If not, he could probably outrun him. The fox's joints squeaked with every move he made.

Tango relaxed. "I'm Tango LaTour. My mistress is Marcellina LaTour, the most beautiful woman in all of Manhattan."

"LaTour? Manhattan?"

"Yes, where all the—" Tango started to explain.

"Never mind." Beau dismissed Tango with a swish of his tail. "Few affairs of the human world either interest or concern me. Humans hurry past all that is good. Too many humans destroy what is beautiful and dear."

Tango cared little for the deep philosophizing of the fox. Also, Tango wasn't sure that he agreed. Augusta was good, and Marcellina was beautiful and ever so dear. However, Tango didn't wish to argue; he was in a hurry to get to the lighthouse.

"You want to go home," Beau remarked.

"How do you know what I want?"

"Little one, I've seen it in your eyes. How, when the sun is shining, you drag a long shadow wherever you go."

Had the fox been spying on him? Why? When?

"I'm waiting for Marcellina to come and take me home."

"Ah, yes, home. And you believe that she will?"

"Of course." Tango hesitated. "I mean, I think she will."

Truth be told, recently Tango had questioned whether Marcellina was, in fact, even searching for her lost dog. Perhaps he'd been no more precious to Marcellina than one of her expensive signature handbags. Marcellina and Diego might've survived the storm and sailed back home—without giving Tango so much as a second thought. Diego probably bought Marcellina a new dog—a dog much smaller, cuter, and far more costly than Tango.

A dog that was "in" this season.

"The moon has waxed and waned since you arrived," noted Beau. Snout up, he studied the deep purple sky, speckled with stars. "Tonight, the moon is full, as it was on the night of the big storm. If your mistress was looking for you, wouldn't she have come by now?"

"What can I do?" Tango whined. "I don't belong here!"

"Maybe I, or someone I know, can help you."

Tango's spirits lifted. "You can? But—how?"

"I'll need time to work it out. Perhaps my dreams will guide me."

The lighthouse beacon flashed on-and-off, on-and-off, beckoning Tango. He raised his paw, ready to take a step. "I'm going to the lighthouse now."

Beau sucked in a breath of air. "I . . . would . . . advise . . . against . . . it."

Beau's tone of voice sent shivers up and down Tango's spine.

"There's no need to hurry, Tango. Trust me," implored the fox. "Wait. Meet me at the lighthouse tomorrow night."

Afraid to discover what Beau Fox feared, Tango abandoned his plan.

Esperanza would have to wait.

CHAPTER 17

An Empty Shed

Greeted by the fresh light of a new day, Augusta felt lighter in spirit than she had for weeks. Like she did each summer, Augusta had transformed her three-season porch into a shop she called One-of-a-Kind.

Wool sweaters, fuzzy scarves, thick mittens, striped socks, crib dolls, sock monkeys, booties, and itty-bitty hats—made with the smallest of stitches and softest of yarns—filled shelves, tables, baskets, and bookcases.

Now she placed a pair of newly knitted argyle socks on a tall stack, stepped back, and admired the fruits of a year's worth of labor.

"I'm ready for the Season, Pup," she announced with a satisfied sigh. "What do you think? How about a walk?"

Pup put his paws over his snout, signaling his disinterest.

Augusta sighed. If only she knew the dog's real name—or where he came from. Or why he goes out into the dark of night, but not into the sunshine of day. The dog *was* a quirky little beast, to be sure, but like many of the young children she used to teach, all the more likeable because of it.

Walking down Main Street toward the post office, Augusta sensed anticipation among the villagers. Soon the playhouse would open—the unofficial start of tourist season in Victoria-by-the-Sea.

Augusta pictured mountains of chocolates filling the glass shelves in Island Chocolates; thick chowder simmering on the stove at Lobsterland; young women in swishy skirts and bright scarves reading tea leaves in Landmark Café; and out-of-school children, eyes sparkling like dragonfly wings in the sun, playing in the street.

Mail in hand, Augusta circled the village, greeting people she'd known all of her life. "Lovely day, isn't it?"

"It is indeed," her neighbors agreed.

Since Pup washed into her life, Augusta had noticed something. Much to her surprise, people seemed more interested in her. Now, she was *the* Miss Gustie who'd rescued a shipwrecked dog and nursed him back to health.

Ambling along, Augusta passed McKenna Skye's

shed. With its sea green walls, butter yellow trim, and rose-colored shutters, the shed looked like a home for whimsical characters that existed only in storybooks.

On a cardboard sign tacked to a stick in the ground, Augusta read the words: "Opening soon." Feeling a little foolish, but unable to stop herself, Augusta peeked through the paned window. Except for a row of glass jars, the shelves were empty. McKenna's sleeping bag was unzipped, but the girl was not in sight.

Probably out walking, Augusta decided, shoulders slumped, hands stuffed into the pouch of her sweatshirt, its tattered hood hiding her face. Always alone, wandering, as if searching for something she might never find.

Seeing the shed that McKenna had so beautifully brought to life devoid of inventory took all the joy out of Augusta's own sense of accomplishment. She experienced a distressing pang of guilt: *candles . . .*

"Wouldn't you just know it," Augusta muttered to herself.

Anyway, just because Augusta knew *how* to make candles—she'd helped her mother often enough— that didn't mean that *she* had to teach a stranger how to make candles, did it?

Yes, yes, Augusta knew that Victoria-by-the-Sea

was the kind of village where friends and neighbors shared what they had, be it food, or goods, or skills, but Augusta was under no obligation, was she?

No, it wasn't her responsibility to teach Big Bart's niece how to make candles—especially *enchanted* candles. She'd never heard of anything so foolish! Tourists could be irritating, but for heaven's sake, they weren't fools! Enchanted candles, indeed.

But later, while bathing Pup, Augusta couldn't get McKenna off her mind. Should she help the girl or not? What with the dog and the shop—she *was* busy, everybody said so, but . . .

Augusta's good heart won out. "Oh, Pup, I've been a mean and selfish old woman," she confessed. "Do unto others . . ."

She rinsed, toweled, and brushed Pup's hair until the strands gleamed like the sand flats on a sunny day. She tied a fringed scarf—melon orange with crocheted buds of purple lupine—around Pup's neck. She hung an "Open in 10 Minutes" sign on her shop door and with Pup at her heels, went to an alcove between the mudroom and the kitchen.

Augusta leaned over and grabbed a brass ring in the floor. "Get back," she warned Pup. "I don't want you falling down these steps; they're steep."

With a strong pull, she lifted a heavy door. Grasping the handrail, she took one step at a time

84

until her right foot landed on the wobbly bottom stair.

How many times had she told herself to fix that stair? Too many to count. . . . She'd do so soon, she vowed.

Rain had seeped through the cellar's stone wall, forming puddles on the floor. Augusta shuddered, pulling her cardigan close.

Ever since she was a child, she'd disliked being down in this dank, dirt-floored cellar. She'd caught mice down here, but feared that she could encounter a rat—like the one she saw, or thought she saw—on the roof of the Pitiful Place last winter.

The rat was big and white, about the same size as Pup. She'd told Bart Cody about the creature, but he'd scoffed, "Gustie Smith, there's no big, white rat living in Old Ada's place. Not anymore."

Now Augusta scanned the shelves, filled with jars of dark red jam and green pickles. With a bristle broom, she whisked away cobwebs. Tiny black spiders scuttled across the stone walls. Pushing aside a row of dust-covered blue canning jars, Augusta spied the cardboard box she was looking for. As she jimmied the box out of the tight space, steel clanked against steel.

Augusta's eyes misted. How she had loved selling candles at the old railroad station with her mother. Holding the box of candle-making equipment with one arm, Augusta trudged up the stairs.

Above her stood Pup—a loyal soldier keeping guard.

"Oh, Pup, what am I getting myself into?" she asked. "What *am* I getting myself into?"

CHAPTER 18

A Simple Heart's Song

Late the next night, Tango—ears erect, eyes alert—made his way to the Victoria lighthouse. The air was chilly, the winds silent. Gentle waves lapped across the sandy shore. In a patch of wild roses, two pale lights flickered.

"Is that you, Beau?" Tango called.

Thorny branches snapped as Beau Fox came into view. "It is."

Much to his surprise, Tango felt no fear. In fact, he was eager to reconnect with his distant kin.

Beau leaned back on his haunches. "Tango, I have considered your situation."

"Tell me! Tell me! I've been waiting all day! Can you help me? Can you?"

Beau reprimanded Tango: "Be still."

Tango willed his body to stop bouncing, but his mind was buzzing.

"If your mistress were looking for you," said Beau thoughtfully, "she would have been here by now."

Tango's ears drooped. "I guess she didn't care about me as much as I thought she did."

"No, no, that's not what I meant," Beau reassured Tango. "Quite the contrary. *I* believe that *she* believes that you are dead."

"She does?"

"When you slipped into the sea, she decided that you would not—that you could not—survive."

"But why?"

"Your rescue *was* a miracle—perhaps your mistress does not believe in miracles."

Tango wasn't sure *he* believed in miracles. He didn't know about Marcellina.

"She does not understand the animal world," Beau said, "where other forces are at work."

Neither did Tango. Tango no longer knew who he was, or where he belonged.

"The night of the storm I heard a voice," explained Beau. "It thundered, 'Save the dog!'"

A voice in Tango's head sneered: *That's nonsense, and you know it.*

"I believe the animals of the sea carried out the command," Beau continued. "Jellyfish banded together under the waves. Their tentacles formed a raft that supported you until the seals woke up and they swam you to shore. Somehow, when the waves broke, you got tangled up in that lobster trap."

Tango's head was spinning. Rescued by seals and jellyfish? A voice that commands the animals of the sea?

"You lived for a reason, so here's what you must do: you must let your beloved know that you are alive—that you wish to come home."

"Why, that's impossible," Tango grumbled. "And you know it! If I were human, I could call Marcellina on the phone, or write her a letter, but—"

"I am talking about hope. Hope is the first step on any significant journey."

"What if Marcellina never comes? What if I have to spend the rest of my life on this island, where I don't belong?"

"I truly believe that your kindred spirit will come looking for you. Perhaps at the moment you least expect it."

"But . . ."

Beau spoke softly. "Hope is a simple heart's song."

With a swish of his tail, the fox slipped out of sight.

Distressed and disheartened, Tango retraced his steps. Above him, tiny, black, web-winged animals soared in confused patterns.

Kindred spirits? Miracles?

"The old fox's brain is addled," Tango muttered.

But as Tango passed under the giant oak in Augusta's backyard, he heard Esperanza whisper: *Without hope . . . without hope . . . nothing . . . is possible.*

CHAPTER 19

Special Deliveries

When Jack Tucker appeared on Augusta's doorstep carrying two large paper bags, Pup didn't bark. Wagging his tail, he sniffed Jack's slacks, his eyes on the vet's pocket, where, Augusta knew, a treat was waiting.

"I got your message," Jack told Augusta. "Since when is Gustie Smith in the business of making candles? I mean, I was glad to pick up the stuff, but . . ."

Jack was waiting for an explanation.

Augusta knew *what* she was doing; what she didn't know was *why*.

He handed off the bags. "Everything you ordered."

"I owe you, Jack."

"I'll put it on your bill." He winked. "Or you could always make me a pot of that lobster chowder Albert always bragged about."

Asparagus needed picking, dishes needed doing, laundry was piling up . . .

"How about tonight, around five?"

"Five it is." Jack smiled.

After Jack left, Augusta waited on a cranky, finicky customer.

Did she look better in a v-neck or a cardigan? Younger in blue, or lavender? Finally, the customer rejected every sweater, leaving them in a heap.

"I can't decide," the customer said. "Maybe I'll come back later."

"Maybe you won't," Augusta muttered as the customer left.

As she loaded the candle-making supplies into a red coaster wagon, Augusta reminded herself to tell McKenna: "Lesson # 1: Tourists are mostly 'just looking.' Get used to it. Learn not to take it personally."

As Augusta pulled the wagon down Main Street, she was surprised, and pleased, to see that Pup was trotting behind. Not only Pup, but also a slobbery, galumphing Newfoundland—twenty times bigger than Pup—named Maggie, who was eagerly sniffing below Pup's tail.

"Shoo! Maggie, shoo!"

Good-naturedly, Maggie sauntered off.

The Enchanted Candles door was closed, but Augusta had a feeling that McKenna was inside.

Augusta knocked. No answer. Augusta knocked again.

"I'm not open," the girl yelled. "Can't you read?"

"It's Augusta Smith. And Pup," Augusta called.

McKenna opened the inner door. Scowling, she peered through the screen. Her eyes dropped to the red wagon. "What the—"

"I must apologize, Miss Skye," explained Augusta, nervously. "You see, I'm not getting any younger, what with the pup and all, well . . ."

Augusta took a deep breath, upset that she was telling a fib. "What I'm trying to say is, I used to make candles." Augusta felt her face redden. "It was a long time ago."

Augusta regarded McKenna through the mesh screen. McKenna's scowl neutralized, but she didn't smile.

"These days," Augusta admitted, "it seems like the more I remember, the more I forget."

McKenna unlatched the screen door. "I don't understand."

Augusta pointed at the brown bags and large cardboard box in the wagon. "Candle-making equipment—with instructions. I believe it's everything you'll need. Candles aren't that hard to make. As I recall, it takes more patience than skill."

Disbelief flooded McKenna's face. She came

93

outside, barefoot, her thin body drowning in a stained, man-size T-shirt.

"I cleaned off the counter and a few shelves in my old barn," Augusta told her. "You're welcome to work out there."

McKenna raked her dark hair, knotting it at the nape of her neck.

"If you need—"

Augusta stopped herself before offering to teach McKenna how to make the candles. McKenna needed to learn to ask for help. No one walks alone.

Tears pooling in her dark gray eyes, McKenna dropped her chin and awkwardly stuck out her hand for a shake. "Hey, thanks a—"

Augusta's wrinkled, veined hand enveloped McKenna's trembling fingers. "You're welcome, my dear."

Looking embarrassed, McKenna dropped to her knees. She stroked Pup's back, hand over hand, swimming across his fur.

"You got yourself a name yet, little dog?"

"Grrrrr . . . ruff!"

Tail erect, Pup broke away and leaped into the wagon bed.

McKenna threw back her head and laughed.

For a moment, Augusta glimpsed what McKenna—who was really quite pretty—may have looked like when she was a very little girl.

Augusta moved her eyes from girl to dog, from dog to girl. It seemed as if she'd started reading two books, both in the middle, without knowing how either story began.

Augusta gave the wagon a good tug.

Somehow, Pup managed to stay onboard until they got home.

CHAPTER 20

The Lighthouse

A week later, at that precious moment between dusk and nightfall, when the sky was neither blue nor black, and the moon had not yet appeared, Beau Fox picked up Tango's scent. Near the lighthouse, Beau found Tango gazing at the blinking beam on top of the square tapered structure.

"I want to go up there," asserted Tango.

"I see. Your sister still calls to you in your dreams."

"Maybe . . . anyhow, I'm tired of wishing. I'm tired of waiting. If Marcellina thinks I'm dead, then I'll find my own way home."

"Indeed . . ."

"You see, Beau, there's this building in Manhattan, so-o-o high, you can see the whole island— parks, rivers, bridges, boats—everything! Once I get to the top of this lighthouse, I'll know where I am. I'll know which way is home."

"Impossible," Beau observed. "Inside, the steel staircase is circular and steep."

"Without hope, nothing is possible."

The fire in Tango's eyes surprised Beau. The night was long. Dinner could wait.

Besides, it wasn't safe for Tango to be out alone at night. Those feral wharf cats had taken to hunting as a pack. But the cats were hunting more for sport than to satisfy their hunger—violating every code of conduct within the animal community.

Beau shuddered. No, Tango had no idea of the dangers that lurked in the animal world. "There is a way to get in," Beau told Tango. "A tight squeeze for me. For you, it should be no problem."

"Let's go!"

With Tango at his heels, Beau took a path through the wild rose patch, across a row of sandstone boulders, and into a muddy gully. Beau scratched at a river of dirt left by recent rains, exposing a hole in a rotting board in the base.

Beau pricked his ears and sniffed the air. No sounds, except for the squeak and chatter of bats leaving their roosts. No recent animal smells, but the odor of humans, who often visited the lighthouse, was thick.

"Before we go in, I must tell you," Beau said. "Wild animals sometimes use this lighthouse as shelter. Unsavory types, like Nigel Stump, scavenge here as well."

Tango acted as if he hadn't heard. "Come on, Beau!"

Once inside, Tango's eyes widened at the sight of the almost-vertical staircase.

"That's more like a ladder. You said there were stairs."

"I warned you."

His one-inch tail held high, Tango raked the floor with his feet. "I've been to the top of the Empire State Building, and I can get to the top of this lighthouse."

The distance between steps was greater than the distance between the pads of Tango's feet and the tips of his ears. Climb to the top? Never, Beau concluded.

Tango appeared undaunted. The little dog squatted underneath the first stair. "Too close," he decided, taking a few steps back. "Here I go!"

Much to Beau's surprise, Tango sprang up, and, for a brief moment balanced on the first step. A split second later, he slipped and tumbled to the floor.

Beau, often burdened by sadness, felt a smile cross his face. By the time Tango plummeted for the fourth time, Beau's skinny old body shook with amusement.

Tango glared at Beau. "You think I can't do this? I'll show you!"

This time, Tango positioned himself even farther back, and, before springing, took a slight running start. Landing on the first step, Tango teetered, quickly adjusted his weight, and stabilized.

"Bravo," Beau said in earnest.

Tango's eyes moved up and down, as if calculating his next maneuver.

Above the whistling of the wind, Beau heard a *tap-tap-tap, tap-tap-tap,* like a tree branch scraping the lighthouse, or claws scratching wood. Beau's eyes shifted, alert to every possibility of danger in this confined space: sprayed by a surprised skunk, slashed by a hostile raccoon.

Beau paced back and forth. "Tango, please, we must leave."

The terrier would not give up, and Beau was loath to leave him alone and unprotected.

Tango made countless unsuccessful attempts. Yet each time he leaped, he took less of a running start, coming closer and closer to the first step until he'd perfected an almost vertical jump. Using the same technique, Tango conquered the second step.

As Tango struggled with the third, Beau lay at the bottom of the staircase, where he remained long into the night, his tired, old body breaking Tango's falls.

CHAPTER 21

Orders from Headquarters

After a day and a night of steady rain, Nigel Stump was lying across a flat rock near the water's edge, covered by a heavy blanket of sunshine. He felt as if he'd never get up again.

Scavenging until dawn had taken its toll. More than ever—and particularly since he'd overheard his friends ridiculing him—Nigel wished that he'd never left home. Hadn't his mother warned him?

"Nigel, you're just like your father," his mother lamented. "One of these days you'll stray too far from home. You'll be sorry. Mark my words."

Earlier, Nigel had tried to sleep in the clubhouse, but a gnawing, sawing sound underneath the Pitiful Place got on his nerves. The huge white rat named Malachi was up to something. If he wasn't chewing on the roof, he was chewing on the stilts. If he wasn't chewing on the ceiling, he was chewing on the floor.

A few days ago, Nigel caught Malachi scurrying up and down the fireplace chimney. "The Pitiful Place is mine to avenge. I will repay," the crazy rodent ranted before it skittered out of sight. How many times had Axel told that rat to stay on the second floor, where he belonged?

"That Malachi is up to no good," Nigel grumbled to Axel.

"He's harmless," Axel replied. "Ugly, maybe, but harmless."

Nigel didn't agree. Malachi was living proof of scientific experimentation gone haywire. Not only was Malachi's body deformed, but his mind was demented. Bottom line: the rat was crazy. Why wouldn't Axel listen?

Now, tiny stones sprayed Nigel's body. "Wake up, Stump."

It was Leftie. Flint was by his side.

Leftie's hazel eyes sparked. "Axel is miffed you weren't around this morning. He told us to round you up. He has an assignment for you."

"Orders from headquarters," said Flint. "Phase Two of the Scram Plan."

A new assignment? Nigel already had two jobs: chief scavenger and night watchman! The other cats, able-bodied, did nothing but eat and sleep—oh, and try to prove how tough they were, hoping that Briar would take notice.

What was Phase One of the Scram Plan? Oh, yeah, THAT.

Lately, the cat pack had been hunting small animals for sport, often not eating their prey. Animals new to the village were their target—easier to catch because they'd had less time to develop a network of secure hiding places and alternate escape routes.

Nigel had been excluded. Pack-hunting required speed; he couldn't keep up with the others. But he also found it despicable. He didn't like outsiders, but hunting for sport went against everything his mother had ever taught him.

Flint interrupted Nigel's thoughts. "Still too much riffraff around this village."

"Way too much," Leftie agreed. "Right, Stump?"

Whiskers twitching, Nigel rose to his feet.

"Here's what you gotta do," said Flint.

Leftie and Flint might be setting him up. Nigel wasn't sure that he trusted them anymore. "Shouldn't I talk to Axel first?"

"Here's the deal," said Flint. "Hunting as a pack isn't as much fun as it used to be."

Leftie rolled his eyes and faked a yawn. "Yeah, been there, done that."

"What's that got to do with me?"

"It's got everything to do with you," snapped Flint. "Your job is to set up some . . . entertainment. Round up pairs of animals—pick two about the same size—and tell them to report to Axel pronto, or else. Axel tells them: 'Either you fight each other, right here, right now, on the clubhouse floor, or you both go down.' "

"We plan to start small," Flint added. "Moles. Chipmunks. A couple of squirrels."

"We take bets on who's going to win." Leftie grinned. "Humans have been doing it for years."

"We pit them against one another?" Nigel's stomach tightened. "Brother against brother? Sister against sister?"

"A fight to the finish," Flint said proudly. "The winner finishes off the loser, and WE finish off the winner."

"Great fun," Leftie agreed. "Don't you get it?"

Nigel felt a chill from the tips of his black ears to the white at the end of his tail. "I get it."

"Start at the bottom of the barrel."

"With who?" Nigel asked.

"The dull, the small, the weak, the stupid, the ugly, the deformed," Flint clarified.

Leftie sneered. "Oh, and don't forget the crippled."

Nigel winced.

"Aw, Stump, Leftie didn't mean it," Flint said. "No, really, skip the crippled. Line up some of these outsiders—you know, the ones who are invading our village."

Leftie stifled a chuckle. "The ones who are invading our shores."

"Like Rat-Boy." Flint snickered.

Leftie must have seen something like doubt cross Nigel's face. Leftie's eyes bored into him. "Unless you can't handle it."

Nigel looked off to the side. Sure, Nigel could handle it, but did he want to? Yeah, Nigel admitted, he'd hoped to encourage animals like Beau Fox and Rat-Boy to find new territory—you know, a couple of pranks, a little bullying, ridicule, that sort of thing—*that's* what Nigel had in mind.

"After all, it *was* your idea," Flint noted. "And, I might add, a big step up for you, Stumpy-Boy."

Maybe Leftie was right. Maybe this was his big break. Do the job right, who knows where this might lead?

"Axel wants the fights to start soon," Flint said.

Leftie swished his tail, impatiently waiting for an answer. "Well . . . ?"

Ultimately, Nigel's ego got the best of him. "No problem." He smirked.

Heads up, tails upright, Leftie and Flint took off.

Now that Nigel saw a better future for himself within the pack, his spirits lifted.

Mole versus mole. Chipmunk versus chipmunk. Squirrel against squirrel.

It was just a game, wasn't it?

CHAPTER 22

One Step at a Time

Beau Fox watched proudly as the little dog con-quered the fourth, fifth, and sixth steps of the steep lighthouse staircase. Once Tango reached the first landing without a misstep, he tackled the second flight of stairs. Going up, Beau observed, took spring and strength. Coming down required bravery and balance.

Beau found himself looking forward to these nightly excursions. Tango was the first animal he'd allowed himself to become close to in all the years since Tawny was killed by the red car.

"Tonight's the night," Tango announced as they trotted toward the lighthouse, eight nights after entering for the first time. "I can feel it in my bones—I'm going all the way to the top!"

Tango revealed his plan. "Tomorrow, we'll sneak in before Big Bart unlocks the door. Doc Tucker keeps talking about the new bridge. Maybe Manhattan's just on the other side."

"Hmm. McKenna once spoke of a long bridge she wanted to cross. But we must hurry," Beau urged. "A storm is brewing."

Thunder rumbled. Filaments of lightning scratched the midnight sky. In the bay, frothy waves churned and slapped against the rocky shore. Gliding on the whistling wind, a squadron of seagulls cawed and cackled with displeasure.

Fear displaced the determination in Tango's eyes. "Let's get out of here!"

"Too late for that," Beau barked. "Go inside! Quick!"

The heavens cracked open. Rain came down in sheets. The two rain-soaked canines crawled into the lighthouse.

Suddenly, a bolt of lightning illuminated the pitch-black interior and a terrifying creature. Beau froze, speechless, mesmerized by a grotesquely misshapen animal—bigger than Tango but smaller than Beau—with dazzling white fur. In the dark, the animal's two beady eyes glowed rose. Tango cowered by Beau's side.

A second bolt of lightning flashed. A long, tapered hairless tail slashed like a knife as it swished across the floor.

"Beau, we've got to get out of here!" Tango cried.

The albino beast opened its jaws; its four front teeth were enormous. The sound that came out of the beast's mouth was neither laughter nor crying, but a freak combination.

"Didn't you hear me, Beau? Run!" commanded Tango. "Now!"

Beau and Tango scrambled out of the lighthouse into the unrelenting rain. They bounded at full speed toward McKenna's shed, where inside a light was burning.

When they were both safe in his tunnel underneath the shed, Beau struggled to catch his breath. Could *that* be the giant rat that haunted the upper floors of the Pitiful Place?

It was big. It was white. What else could *IT* be?

Beau hadn't believed that the monstrous rat truly existed. The cats, he figured, had fabricated the phantom creature. What better way to keep other animals out of their space?

"What was that—that *thing*?" asked Tango.

Beau panted and wheezed. "A . . . very . . . large . . . disfigured . . . rat."

"I'm not sure that makes me feel any better."

A pain stabbed Beau's chest—a grim reminder that his days were numbered. Beau squeezed his eyes and waited for the pain to pass.

"Now what?" Tango complained. "We can't go in the lighthouse again—not if that huge rat is there."

Beau didn't say anything. At the moment, he was too tired to deal with the often self-centered little terrier and the dog's single-minded determination to go back home.

A wave of sympathy and understanding washed across Tango's face. "How old are you, Beau?" he asked softly.

"Why do you ask?"

"Old? Or old-old?"

"Old enough to be one of the oldest foxes on the island, I imagine," Beau answered. "I've seen fifteen summers."

"How long do foxes usually live? Do they live as long as dogs?"

"Fourteen summers, it is said."

"But, but that means—"

"Do not worry. My time has not yet come. And when it does, it will be a welcome journey."

"I don't understand."

"You will, Tango. In your own time, you will."

CHAPTER 23

No One Walks Alone

Stand up straight, speak up, brush your hair out of your eyes. That's what Augusta wanted to say when she opened her shop door and found McKenna standing there. Instead, Augusta waited patiently as McKenna hemmed and hawed, shifting her weight from one foot to the other.

"Miss Gustie, uh, you know . . ."

"Yes?"

"You know how you gave me all the candle stuff, I mean, you and Doc Tucker, and you said that the instructions were in the bag, and they were, but . . ."

"Yes?"

McKenna's lower lip quivered. "The thing is, I'm not the best reader, and—"

"You're finding it hard to follow the instructions?"

"Pretty hard. I mean, I understand most of what I'm supposed to do, but—"

"You could use some help?" Augusta asked. "Certainly."

"But you'll only need to tell me once. I'm a fast learner," added McKenna eagerly. "I put everything out in the barn, like you told me."

"Meet me out there at nine, after I close up shop. Bring a couple of Bart's hurricane lanterns from the wharf—we'll need some light. And the longest extension cord he's got, for the electric burner."

"Okay." The girl nodded.

"And tie back your hair, for heaven's sake, or you'll catch us both on fire."

⬿

Augusta's small barn had once housed a team of horses, a wagon, a pony, and a buggy. These days it held a lawn mower, gardening tools, and a wooden dory that leaked. Barn owls, bats, and pigeons took refuge in the rafters.

"Like I said before," Augusta began, "candle making takes more patience than skill. Patience and practice. You can't expect perfection on your first try."

"No, ma'am."

"No need to call me ma'am—makes me feel older than I already am."

Suddenly, a smile broke on McKenna's face. "Oh, look!"

111

McKenna pointed at Pup, who was curled into a ball up on top of a stool. "How'd he get up there?"

"Sometimes I think that Pup's part monkey," Augusta said. "Why, the other day, I found him on top of my dresser, pawing through my jewelry box. Every time I turn around, he's sticking his nose into something."

"That's weird. Have you decided what you're going to call him?"

"Well, now," Augusta said, wanting to stick to business. "Step number 1: We need to prime the wicks. Use the double boiler there. In the bottom half, add a couple of inches of water. Use the garden hose. Next, bring it to a boil."

Once McKenna got the water boiling, Augusta continued. "You pick out the size mold you want, and I'll show you how to measure the wick."

McKenna chose an octagonal steel mold. Augusta shook her head. "Too hard for a beginner. Try a round one."

McKenna chose a cylinder about seven inches tall.

"Good. Now, melt a little paraffin wax in the top of the double boiler, about this much." With her fingers, Augusta measured one inch. "Leave the wicks to soak in the wax for five minutes—set the timer. Then we have to let them dry."

Augusta told McKenna to hold on; she hustled off to get a cookie sheet from her kitchen cupboard.

When Augusta came back, McKenna asked, "Should I cover the sheet with anything?"

"Yes, good thinking. Cover the sheet with that greaseproof paper—there, in that bag of stuff Doc Tucker bought you."

Step by step, Augusta showed McKenna the entire candle-making process in a way not unlike the way she may have taught a curious kindergartner. Pup was attentive to their every move. Augusta was relieved that he was sticking close to home. His mysterious disappearances at night were terribly upsetting.

"I'm going to make my candles Prince Edward Island colors," McKenna announced, plucking wicks from the molten wax with a tweezers.

"And what colors are those?"

"Coral, like the sunset. Pink, like wild roses. Purple, like lupine, and—"

"Three is enough," Augusta cautioned. "Each color requires a new batch of wax, remember. You'll have to experiment to find the exact shade. Mother used to say . . ."

"You used to make candles with your mom?" asked McKenna, wistfully.

"Oh, yes."

An awkward silence filled the space between them.

Augusta knew she shouldn't pry, but before she realized it, the question was asked: "And where, may I ask, is *your* mother?"

"Since I don't know *who* my mother is, it's hard to say where she is."

"I'm sorry," Augusta said quietly.

As much as she wanted to ask about McKenna's father, Augusta couldn't think of a tactful way to question the girl further. She picked up the wax thermometer. "It's time to test the temperature. When the melted wax is ninety-three degrees Celsius, it's ready."

McKenna dipped the thermometer into the wax. After waiting a minute, she held the thermometer up to the light. "Nope, not hot enough," McKenna concluded.

McKenna petted Pup, keeping her eye on her work. "I'm part Mi'kmaq, you know."

"Why, no, I didn't know."

"Annie Pike told me I was, and I believe her. Even if I'm not, I want to be."

"It seems you either are, or you aren't."

"Yeah, I know. I mean, I want to practice their ways. The Earth would be a better place if we all did. That's what I think."

"And who is Annie Pike?"

"Annie was my second—no, my third foster mother. Annie was Mi'kmaq. She swore I was Mi'kmaq, too—she could feel it in her soul. Annie didn't care what some county record said about me."

"Your second or third foster mother? How many have you had?"

"Oh, after Annie moved to Toronto—that's where I'm going, by the way—let's see." McKenna counted with her fingers. "Seven."

Augusta shook her head. The very idea that this young girl had lived in—how many?—foster homes was appalling.

"You're going to Toronto?" A vision of homeless girls living on the streets—hungry and desperate—sent shivers up and down Augusta's spine.

"Yup, at the end of the summer. After I make enough money selling candles."

"Do you have relatives there?"

"No."

"Are you going to live with Annie Pike?"

"Um, maybe. But don't tell anyone—you won't, will you? Promise?"

Augusta didn't know exactly what to say, but she knew better than to make any such promise. Perhaps teaching McKenna how to make candles—and money—wasn't such a good idea after all.

But Augusta couldn't back out now—certainly not tonight.

"Is the wax ready?" Augusta asked.

McKenna nodded.

"Pour it into the center of the mold. Don't let any wax splash on the sides. Yes, that's right. Good job."

As it turned out, Augusta never gave an instruction more than once. Finally, when Augusta was all but sleeping on her feet, McKenna shrieked, "Look!" A candle slid out of its mold. "I did it! I did it!"

McKenna clapped like a toddler who'd blown out all the candles on her birthday cake. For a moment, Augusta saw herself when she was McKenna's age—tall, skinny, uncomfortable in her own skin. But loved . . . yes, Augusta had been loved.

"That's a good night's work, McKenna." Augusta yawned. "Mother always said that the hardest part is cleaning up, so we'd better get to it."

"Can we make one more?"

"No, I think that's enough for one night."

"Please, please, please, Miss Gustie?"

"Oh, all right," she conceded. "One more."

McKenna didn't ask for help, but her eyes sought Augusta's approval every step of the way.

Finally, the long night came to an end. Augusta put Pup in her arms. Before leaving, Augusta paused, dying to ask McKenna just one more question: What—exactly—makes these candles *enchanted*?

CHAPTER 24

Enchanted Candles

After days and nights of practice—wicks too long, dye too dark, wax that wouldn't harden—McKenna had molded thirteen pillar candles.

Into the hot paraffin she'd added threads of silver birch bark, purple lupine blossoms, and scrapings from the inside of blue mussel shells. She'd stirred the mixture with a heron's tail feather for good luck.

Now, on the night before she would (finally!) open for business, McKenna practiced writing a set of instructions on squares of colored cardstock that Miss Gustie had given her. If customers were to believe that a candle possessed mystical powers, they'd expect a way to invoke its magic.

First, McKenna wrote: *At midnight, on the night of the new moon, light the enchanted candle. Make a wish. Repeat every night until the next new moon.*

No, that didn't seem mysterious enough. Maybe it should rhyme: *Enchanted candle, burning flame, see my wish, say my name.*

No, that didn't make any sense, although she liked the way it sounded.

Then McKenna tried: *Enchanted candle, burning bright, grant the wish I wish tonight.* Not bad, but nothing special. Plus, it sounded like *Twinkle, twinkle, little star.*

In the end, McKenna ripped up every card she'd written. Instructions were like a guarantee. What if a customer came back, called her a fraud, and demanded a refund? No, best not to put anything in writing. Name the candles, hope for the best.

After McKenna named each candle—*Tangerine Moon, Sunset Song, Violet Night*—McKenna penciled the price in the corner of a name tag. With yarn from Miss Gustie's scrap bag, she tied the name tag to the candle.

Enchanted or not, the candles were pretty cool. But were they truly enchanted? Did she herself believe in their power?

Early the next morning, unable to sleep, McKenna roamed the village. A crimson cardinal whistled a greeting, mourning doves cooed. A big, burly black dog made its morning rounds, marking its territory.

Windows yellowed with light; fishermen hustled toward their patient boats.

At exactly nine o'clock, she took a deep breath. Almost sick with excitement, she hung the "Open" sign. A few tourists walked past, commented on the shed's cuteness, but didn't come in. Two Japanese girls snapped pictures of Enchanted Candles, but didn't come in either. A couple of the Cody kids hung around until McKenna shooed them away. The hours dragged. By noon, McKenna's fingernails were ragged.

McKenna's first customer—a young woman with thick-framed black glasses—picked up a rosy orange candle. "So, what do I do? Just light it—poof! My wish comes true?" She wrinkled her nose, shaking her head. "Not."

Palms sweating, McKenna recalled watching Annie Pike light sweet grass. McKenna struck a match and lit the *Dream Melon* candle. "First, fan the smoke toward your heart," McKenna murmured, hoping to sound mysterious. McKenna forgot what Annie used to do next, so she improvised. "Then, bow your head, like this, and make a wish. Gaze into the flame for exactly thirteen seconds."

Thirteen seconds seemed like a long time when someone you didn't know was watching you. "Hold the candle in front of you, swirl three times, and—"

"All right, already," the young woman said. "I'll take it. I don't believe it's enchanted, but the color's awesome."

McKenna's second customer, a plain-looking woman, with an even plainer daughter—maybe eight years old—wandered into the shop. A man with a bulldoglike face came in, too, but after a quick glance, walked out.

Immediately, the straw-haired girl picked up a candle called *Peppermint Joy*. With her freckled hands, she rubbed the cherry pink and white candle as if it were Aladdin's lamp. "Is it really enchanted? If I make a wish, will it come true?"

Usually, lies came easily to McKenna, but somehow, she couldn't bring herself to lie to this little girl.

"It's very pretty, but come, Cecilia," said her mother. "There are other shops in the village I'd like to see."

"Any wish? Any wish at all?" the girl asked.

Something that Doc Tucker said when McKenna thanked him for buying the supplies came to mind: "The way I figure, the first step in getting what you want is naming it—knowing what it is you want in the first place. Most folks have hearts full of wanting, but not the right words. Seems like these candles might force them to decide what they want, and once they do, they'll be well on their way to getting it."

"I don't know for sure," answered McKenna. "But I'll tell you what I do know."

"Is it a story?"

"I guess you could say so." McKenna nodded.

"Mom, she's going to tell me the story of the enchanted candle! Can I stay and listen? Please?"

"It's a short story," McKenna told Cecilia's mother. "You can sit on the bench."

"Fine." She sighed. "Perhaps it is time to take a break."

"One Christmas morning, when I was a little girl— about your age—I saw a sea green dollhouse with yellow shutters in a catalogue. I wrote Santa Claus a letter and told him that I wanted that dollhouse more than anything in the world."

McKenna's voice cracked. She squeezed her eyes, hoping to dam up the tears that wanted to escape. "I didn't get it. On Christmas morning, I was so mad—or disappointed, I guess—that I ran upstairs and locked myself in the attic. And look what I found?"

"It's a Bible!"

McKenna opened the tattered book to the page where her recipe was tucked. "See," McKenna pointed, "it's the recipe for my enchanted candles."

Cecilia's eyes widened. "Wow-y, zow-y."

"Honest, Cecilia, I don't know if my candles are enchanted or not. But once upon a time, I wished for a sea green house with yellow shutters, and this summer, my wish came true!"

"I believe they are enchanted!" Cecilia exclaimed. She fingered the name tag. "Mom, will you buy me *Peppermint Joy*? Please?"

The mother paid McKenna and joined the man, who was pacing and smoking, outside. McKenna wrapped the candle in sky blue tissue with a lavender grosgrain ribbon, like the kind Miss Gustie used in her shop.

Cecilia held her mother's present up to her heart. "We're going back home to Vancouver tomorrow, but I'll come back next year—I promise—and tell you whether my wish came true."

"That'd be cool."

"Want to know what I'm going to wish for?"

"Only if you want to tell me," McKenna answered.

Cecilia cupped her freckled hand around her mouth and whispered, "I want my mom and dad to quit fighting."

Stunned, McKenna nodded, and the pale girl slipped away.

CHAPTER 25

Low Tide

One night, during the third ferocious storm of the summer, the entire village of Victoria-by-the-Sea lost its power. Tango heard Augusta close the book she'd been reading. She lit two table candles and placed them on her desk, in front of a window that faced the sea. Then Augusta drew Tango, who was trembling, onto her lap.

"I'm right here, Pup," Augusta assured him. "Don't be afraid."

Tango gazed at the rain-slicked window. Light from the candles reflected off the pane. If he cocked his head one way, there were two flames, but from another angle, there were four. Spellbound, he watched the flames dance on glass.

Suddenly, a glimpse of the last time he'd seen Marcellina appeared in Tango's mind: the look of horror on Marcellina's face as he slid off Diego's sailboat into the sea. How she screamed "Tango! Tango!! TANGO-O-O-O!" and prepared to dive. How Diego pulled her back into the storm-tossed boat.

Oh, how could Tango ever have doubted her love? She'd been willing to risk her life to save him! Now, more than ever, he must—he simply must— find a way home.

But how?

It would take . . . a miracle. . . .

Tango hopped off Augusta's lap and dashed to the mudroom.

"Pup! Come back here!" Augusta called, but by then Tango was already out the door.

The storm ended as abruptly as it had begun. Tango crisscrossed the rain-soaked grass, sniffing for Beau's most recent scent marker. Once located, he followed Beau's trail toward a rocky point that jutted into Victoria Bay.

Since the morning he'd washed ashore, Tango had yet to come this close to the sea. He was terrified.

Tango took a deep breath, inspired by Marcellina's courage. "You are strong, brave, and fearless." Tango lifted his chin. "You won the war with the waves and escaped a watery grave." He puffed out his chest. "You conquered the lighthouse stairs."

Finally, before all the gods and spirits and kings of the sea, he declared: "You are the TANGO!"

Tango hurried along.

In the moonless night, Beau's body was a shadowy black silhouette against the dark gray sky. Beau, Tango realized, was poised on the bow of a beached boat.

Suddenly his courage weakened. The odor of rotting wood, kelp, and dead sea life overpowered him. In his mind, his little body was bobbing in a frothy, churning, crazy sea.

"Beau!" he croaked. "It's me, Tango."

"Do not be afraid, my friend," Beau called back. "Come. Be with me."

"How am I supposed to get up there?"

"Go around to *Morningstar*'s other side. Any dog who scaled the steel bones inside the lighthouse will find a way."

Tango, anxious to seek Beau's advice, bounded up the boat's back side, taking a few tumbles before making it to the top.

"Beau, guess what?"

"Shhh . . ." Beau admonished. "It is a beautiful night."

Tango raised his snout. A million silver stars sparkled like sequins on a black gown.

As if revealing a precious secret, Beau whispered into Tango's ear, "We foxes believe that when our

126

body dies, its spirit soars to the sky and becomes a star."

"You do?"

"No one knows how long this takes," Beau said. "Since her death, I have been waiting for Tawny's star to appear." Beau sighed contentedly. "At last, I see her."

"Speaking of seeing her—"

"Hush!" Beau hissed. "She is asking me to join her in the Land of Stars. She is begging me to come home."

"Speaking of home—"

Abruptly, with a fierce flick of his tail, Beau turned his back on Tango.

Tango cringed, closed his eyes, and let the wind play with his fur. If only, Tango wished, the silver stars would make a path that Tango could follow back to the island of Manhattan.

After a few silent minutes, Tango took a fleeting look at the bay, which, he quickly realized, was empty. "Beau!" Tango gasped. "The water—it's gone!"

"The sea is at low tide. Have you not noticed this phenomenon before? Between the rising and setting of the sun, and again at night," explained Beau, "the moon pulls the water close. Think about it, Tango. This bay is where you slipped into the sea— the same angry body of water, now at peace."

Beau paused, looking at Tango with eyes filled

with concern. "If only your heart was at peace—if only you could accept that you were brought here for a reason."

"I know why I ended up here. I fell off a boat."

Beau shook his head.

Sometimes Beau seemed amused by Tango, which Tango found slightly irritating.

As Tango considered the dark, desolate stretch of sand, an idea crystallized. *Perhaps . . . perhaps . . .*

"Beau, do you think my silver collar might be somewhere out there?"

"What silver collar?"

"I thought I told you. . . . When I fell off Diego's boat, I was wearing a collar made of silver links, with a silver heart attached."

"Yes, I know collars. Like the other dogs in the village wear."

"Well, yes, but much nicer," bragged Tango. "Marcellina bought it at an expensive store."

Beau seemed perplexed. "And?"

"The heart had my name on one side and Marcellina's on the other. Her address and phone number, too. In case I got lost. An identification tag."

"This is the first I've heard of such silver."

"I figured it was at the bottom of the sea. But now I'm not so sure. I've been looking around Augusta's house—her yard, too—just in case."

"And?"

"I can't find it." Tango glanced again at the near-empty bay. "Will you help me look? Please? Please?"

"Not now, my friend."

"Then I'll go myself."

"No, Tango, you must not. The tide is returning. Incoming tides can catch you unaware. Never, NEVER, go out there alone at night. It's too dangerous."

"Tomorrow then! What time?"

"I cannot search the sand flats with you during the day. I am a fox. I must stay out of sight." Beau chuckled. "The humans, I think, confuse me with a wolf—they are afraid that I will eat their children."

"Come on, Beau," Tango begged. "Please?"

"At low tide, humans walk there, gathering seashells, digging for clams. Their children splash in puddles and build castles. You will be safe."

"No, I'd better not," Tango said. "Purebred dogs like me get stolen all the time in New York."

"I doubt that anyone will take you, but if you really are afraid, go with McKenna Skye. She often walks out there. She, too, is looking for something."

"Won't she think I'm weird, following her around like that?"

"McKenna has a gift. She will understand."

"You mean, I can talk to her—like I'm talking to you—and she'll know what I'm saying?"

"Maybe." Beau nodded. "Unfortunately, McKenna's powers are good only if she herself believes she possesses them." The fox sighed. "Many gifts are like that."

"Like me and the lighthouse steps?"

"Yes, quite similar. Tomorrow, watch for McKenna. Stay by her side."

Beau leaped off the side of the overturned boat. His landing was unsteady, and Tango heard bone grinding against bone. The fox was moving slowly, too. Tango pictured the leftovers waiting for him in his bowl in Augusta's kitchen and ran ahead of his friend.

When Tango looked over his shoulder, he discovered that three cats had circled Beau, blocking his way. Tango's body tensed. Although he couldn't hear the words, Tango sensed hostility. Keeping his eyes on Beau, Tango pulled himself up to his full height, tail raised, skin tingling.

A black cat with a long tail pawed at the air, its claws extended. Beau snapped his jaw, followed by a series of staccato barks. Cat hisses scraped the quiet night like knives across steel. The cats moved in closer, then backed off, moved in closer, backed off. Baring his teeth, Beau stood his ground.

Tango would have to fight; he had no choice. The old fox couldn't handle these cats alone. Tango was about to spring into action, but froze.

Pssst! A one-eared cat with blazing eyes spit in Beau's face. Beau screamed. Tango's blood curdled. Beau pounced upon the orange cat's tail as if it were prey, bit hard, and twisted. The orange cat broke free, and in an instant, the three cats stalked off.

"Whew!" Tango released the air trapped in his lungs, relieved that his courage was not to be tested.

At least not tonight.

CHAPTER 26

McKenna's Gift

After tending the shop for twelve hours, McKenna had sold seven of her thirteen enchanted candles. She sat on the bench and counted the money she'd made: 3 tens, 4 fives, and 5 ones. Except for the twenty dollars she planned to give Jeannie Cody for groceries, the rest was all profit. Doc Tucker told McKenna she could wait a few weeks before paying him back.

The lights were still on at Miss Gustie's. She'd go over and thank her. Without Miss Gustie, McKenna would have nothing.

Before going, McKenna erased the price and then wrapped the candle named *Lilac Cloud*. Just in case one of the Cody kids had sticky fingers, she locked the door.

"I didn't sell anything, not a single sweater," Miss Gustie lamented after McKenna arrived. "A tall woman came in, bigger than me, and found a sweater she loved—that red sweater there—but she needed it in a size 44, and I only had a 36.

"Then a tiny bit of a woman came in. She wanted the blue sky pattern in size 36, but I only had a 44. And so it went, all the day long—my worst day yet. If I have too many more days like this, Pup and I will both be eating dog chow."

McKenna hung her pouch on the back of a kitchen chair and sat down.

"So, how did you do?" Miss Gustie finally asked.

McKenna felt her face flush. She wanted to gush out her good news, but after hearing Miss Gustie's complaints, she held back. "Okay, I guess. Listen, I can't stay long. I have to make some more candles." McKenna held out her gift. "But here. I brought you something—for helping me."

Miss Gustie's face brightened as she untied the ribbon. "Is it enchanted? Enchanted enough to make my sweaters fly off the shelves?"

"If you believe it is, then it is. That's what Doc Tucker says."

"Why, thank you, McKenna." Miss Gustie folded the tissue paper, smoothing it into a neat square. "What a nice surprise. Now, don't hold out on me, how many candles did you sell?"

"Seven." McKenna beamed.

"Good for you."

The gray-haired woman smiled as if she truly meant it—kind of like a grandma might, McKenna thought.

"You should feel real proud of yourself," said Miss Gustie.

McKenna quickly shooed away the vision of having a grandmother.

"You know," she told Miss Gustie, "it's almost like I knew which candle they'd choose before they did. Spooky, huh?"

"Yes, I know how that is sometimes."

Since Miss Gustie seemed in no hurry for her to leave, McKenna told her about her first customer and the ritual she'd improvised.

"Oh, it gives me the shivers just thinking about you playing around with a person's dreams like that."

"Except for one little girl," explained McKenna, "no one else even asked if they were really enchanted. One lady bought one because it matched her bathroom."

"And what did you say to the little girl?" asked Miss Gustie.

"I told her the truth."

"And what is the truth?"

"That I didn't know."

Miss Gustie released a deep breath, nodding her approval.

∞

Hours later, inside her shed, McKenna pulled the ceiling bulb chain. In the dark, she twisted the strands of her hair, afraid to vocalize her real fear: What if her candles really were enchanted?

Sitting cross-legged on the floor, she lit the willow green candle she'd named *Mint Dreams*.

What if the flame lights up my future?

McKenna fanned the smoke up, down, and around: heart, mind, soul, and body.

What if the flame lit up the past?

Dreams fluttered close to her heart, but she couldn't put her wishes into words. She concentrated, gazing into the flame, counting: *One thousand and one, one thousand and two, one thousand and three . . .*

No! Forget it! She—whoever *she* is—didn't—doesn't—care about me, and I don't care about her. A deep breath filled her cheeks; when she blew out the air, a shower of spit came with it. The flame sizzled and died.

McKenna buried her head in her hands. Beneath the floorboards, she heard a soft, soulful crooning, the fox's lullaby. Knowing that the fox was close gave her comfort.

McKenna lit a second candle, a deep pink one called *Wild Rose*. She peered into the flame, trying to see herself living in Toronto, Annie Pike's arm resting on her shoulder.

But no matter how long she gazed at the flickering light, McKenna could only see what she already had: a shed, the fox, Miss Gustie, and the little dog, Pup.

CHAPTER 27

Encounter with a Twenty-Three-Legged Cat

In the corner of Augusta's bountiful garden, the raspberry bushes had sent their stems under the fence, into the Cody backyard. Ripe berries hung there like little red lanterns from the green stems.

On his way to see Beau, Tango popped one raspberry after another into his mouth. Full of a fresh fruit long forbidden by Marcellina, Tango crawled into Beau's tunnel beneath Enchanted Candles.

In the dark, he sought Beau's amber eyes.

"I'm burrowing a den for the winter," explained Beau. "This winter, I will not sleep in my den in the dunes. Even if McKenna returns to the North Shore, I will not follow."

Tango didn't have to ask why. Beau's reddish gray fur was thinning; Tango could almost count Beau's ribs. Often, Beau was short of breath. Saddened, Tango envisioned Beau alone all winter in this cold, dark hole.

What would Tango do if Beau were to die? He'd grown accustomed to being with Beau. Did that mean that he and Beau were kindred spirits? And what about McKenna Skye? Why was Beau so loyal to the tall girl with the long black hair? What was their story? If Tango asked, would Beau tell him?

Above them, a door closed. A key turned in a lock.

"That's McKenna," said Beau. "On her way to the sand flats. It's almost low tide. Follow her."

"I can't, I told you. I hardly know her!"

"You have nothing to fear."

"She'll think I'm lost. She'll pick me up and take me back to Miss Gustie's."

"Tango, she will understand. Do not worry."

Tango rubbed his snout with his paw, hesitant to make the move.

"Do as I say," Beau urged. "Hurry!"

Tango scooted across the Codys' disheveled yard, scurried across Water Street, past the lighthouse, through spears of bright green beach grass. Sitting on a weathered log on the pebbly side of the beach, McKenna was unlacing her boots. Her gleaming black hair was pulled back into a pony tail.

"Hey, little dog, what are you doing here? Does Miss Gustie know you're out here?"

Tango blinked. He blinked again. He couldn't

believe his eyes. A shiny chain of silver links encircled McKenna's ankle!

Darting as close as he dared, Tango growled, then barked frantically. *That's my collar! That's my collar! Do you hear me? It's mine!*

A puzzled look clouded McKenna's face. "What the heck is the matter with you?"

Tango pounced on her ankle and nipped at the silver links.

McKenna pushed him away. "Stop it! You are the silliest dog I've ever seen."

Tango circled McKenna, inching his way closer to her ankle. Was his silver heart attached?

"It's okay. Come here, little guy. I'm sorry I pushed you."

While his head was telling him to attack—to rip his silver chain off McKenna's leg—the voice of his sweet sister, Dulcinea, spoke to his heart: *Be kind, Tango.*

McKenna's eyes were dark brown—not unlike his own—and kind, like Marcellina's. She did seem to be trying to understand what he wanted. Calmed, Tango wagged his tail. While McKenna rubbed his ears, Tango smelled the ring of silver that once connected his silver heart to the chain. The ring had a tiny gap between the ends, where his identification tag must have slipped through.

McKenna petted his head. "You're a nice little dog, even if you are a little weird. Someday I'm going to get myself a dog just like you. Maybe I'll name him Nipper."

It had been a long time since anyone actually said to him that he was a nice little dog. Tango licked her hand. For a moment, it felt as if a butterfly was beating its fragile wings inside his heart.

"Do you want to come with me?"

Tango barked with joy. Of course he did!

McKenna took long strides across the flats, keeping her eyes on the sand. Tango was amazed— McKenna must know what he wanted!

At first Tango followed in McKenna's footsteps. However, hope and impatience got the best of him; he split off to carry on his own search. Tango made wider and wider circles around McKenna, looking for clues.

Overcome by a delicious sense of freedom, Tango soon lost focus. He splashed in tide pools, rolled, and turned somersaults in the sand. He scampered away from water spouts made by razor clams and chased skittering crabs off flat rocks.

McKenna raced after him, laughing. When she caught up, Tango shook his body, splattering water all over her legs. Again she laughed.

All of a sudden, out of the corner of his eye,

Tango spied a purple blob in the sand. He lifted his paw, ready to examine the unfamiliar creature.

McKenna cautioned him away. "That's a jelly-fish."

A jellyfish? When he went overboard, a school of jellyfish kept him afloat—isn't that the story Beau told him? This gooey creature? But how?

"The jellyfish is stuck," explained McKenna. "It has to wait until the tide rolls back in and washes its body back to sea. Else, it'll die."

But this jellyfish had possibly saved his life! How could Tango just let it die?

Tango laid his head on his paws and whined.

"I know. It breaks my heart to see any animal die without a fighting chance." McKenna bent down and took a closer look. "Go on! Run! Have fun! Let me worry about the jellyfish."

Trusting that McKenna would care for the stranded sea animal, off he sped. Now he was the World's Fastest Terrier. Wind rustled his untrimmed fur. He sprinted from the nose of one sand bar to the tail of the next and swam through rivulets of water between. How glorious he felt! How free!

Finally, Tango got winded. He stopped to catch his breath. Where was McKenna?

In the distance, McKenna appeared as a black speck near the wharf. Alone, and very far from shore, Tango felt small and insignificant, overpow-ered by the wide expanse of sand between him and the safety of Augusta's house.

He ran at full speed toward shore, but abruptly braked as a foul odor wafted in the breeze. He sniffed the air. Cats.

"Well, well, well." Tango heard a raspy, unfamil-iar voice. "If it isn't the Rat-Boy."

Tango spun around. A black-and-white cat with three legs, a black beard, and a white tip at the end of his tail approached.

"Hey, Rat-Boy, long time no see."

Before Tango could react, he was hemmed in by one, two, three, four, five other cats. Beau's whis-pered description of how the cats were terrorizing small animals flashed in his mind. Would they attack him, right here in broad daylight?

"What-cha up to, Rat-Boy?" smirked the creamy blue cat, one of three who'd surrounded Beau some nights back.

Tango was terrified—more so than he'd been of the humongous white rat. In this pack, Tango sensed something far more deformed, much more sinister. Although each cat was individually sized, shaped, and colored, what emerged was a single gruesome creature with six tails, twelve eyes, and twenty-three legs. Their voice was one voice. Their objective: to instill fear.

"Looking for something?" snarled the tabby.

"I might be," Tango answered, trying not to appear unnerved.

But his body betrayed him: the hackles on his back spiked, a growl rose in his throat.

The Beast sneered and jeered with all six of its mouths.

"You hear that, Nigel?—he's looking for something. In your territory." The midnight black cat snickered.

"Yeah, Nigel, maybe you should make the Rat-Boy your Assistant Scavenger," mocked an ivory and taupe cat with crystal blue eyes.

More hoots and howls.

The big orange cat with the sinister face circled Tango. The cat's breath smelled like a New York sewer.

Tango shifted his weight to his back legs, preparing to attack.

WHACK! SMACK! A plate of steel slapped the sand.

"Scram!" McKenna Skye's voice rang out.

Tango sprang out of the cat circle. He didn't stop running until he was dozens of yards away.

Again McKenna slapped the blade of her shovel on the sand. "Like I said: SCRAM!"

The cats sped off. McKenna heaved an aluminum pail into the middle of the retreating pack.

"EEeeeee-Ow!" the blue cat wailed when the pail bounced off her back.

In a blink of an eye, the Cat-Beast raced toward the wharf, all six tails tucked between its twelve back legs. Tango ran toward McKenna and begged to be picked up.

"It's okay. They're gone now." She tucked Tango under her arm and with her free hand, gathered up the pail and shovel.

McKenna paused. She seemed to be puzzling out what had just occurred. She shrugged her shoulders. "Come on. We'd better get back, or Miss Gustie will be sending out a posse to find you. She'll have my hide if she thinks it was my idea to bring you out here. We can rescue jellyfish tomorrow."

CHAPTER 28

Putting the Pieces Together

Deep in his ever-lengthening tunnel underneath Enchanted Candles, Beau Fox slept. Beau dreamed that he was hunting in a thick stand of spruce. Sunbeams cut through the branches, and suddenly, Beau was knee-deep in a garden of pink flowers, lady's slippers in bloom.

With slipper-shaped lips, the chorus of flowers implored him to lie down in their heavenly bouquet. But he wasn't ready. Or was he? Then, on the far side of the garden, Tawny appeared. Her fur—once red—was silvery white, sparkling with teardrops of dew.

Just when Beau thought that he could resist the invitation no longer, Tango burst into his den. "Beau! Beau! Wake up! Wake up! You aren't going to believe it!"

Beau opened his sleep-heavy eyelids.

Seeing Tango's eyes shining with excitement, Beau was reminded that he still had work to do. That somehow this kinship was working for the greater good.

"Beau! Beau!" Tango yapped. "Are you listening?"

Beau heaved a sigh. "Yes, Tango, I'm listening."

"McKenna Skye has my silver collar! McKenna has my collar—I saw it!"

"The chain that held your silver heart?"

"Yes! Yes!"

"How can you be sure? Certainly such items are common enough among humans, and—"

"No! It's mine!" Tango insisted. "You've known McKenna all her life—has she always worn a silver chain around her ankle?"

"No, I cannot say that I have seen such a chain. But—she keeps herself well covered."

"I want it back."

Beau closed his eyes. A memory returned. The bay. The calm after the storm. The lobster trap. He'd been in the wild rose thicket, watching.

The beach. McKenna digging. Nigel scratching.

Perhaps Tango was onto something. Maybe . . . McKenna had found Tango's silver link collar. Maybe . . . Nigel Stump had found the heart-shaped charm.

Was it possible?

If so, it would be so simple. Get the silver collar. Get the silver heart. Tango gets identified, Tango goes home.

Tears veiled Beau's eyes. In his mind, he saw Tango and Tawny standing side by side in a garden of pink flowers, both out of reach. Unless—

"Beau, Beau! Are you going to help me, or not?"

"I'm sorry, Tango. Let us go into the sunshine."

Beau felt deeply conflicted. Didn't Tango realize how good he had it here? How much he meant to Miss Gustie? How much Tango meant . . . to him?

Tango followed Beau along a barb-wired fence, where rose red fireweed sparkled, lupine lined the ditch, and daisies, bluebells, and buttercups flowered among the weeds. Weary and out of breath, Beau fashioned himself a bed in the long, sun-warmed grasses.

"Tango, this is what I remember: the morning you washed ashore, I saw McKenna pull something shiny out of the sand. I thought nothing of it. She put it in her pocket. Later, Nigel Stump came and scratched the sand where she'd been standing. When Nigel lifted his head, he had something in his mouth. When he saw me, he took off."

"Are you sure? Are you positive?"

"Enough!" Beau said in a voice laced with exasperation.

"Beau, please," begged Tango. "Let's go find Nigel—now."

"Not so fast. . . . We need a plan."

Rising, Beau glared at Tango. "Do not—I repeat—DO NOT approach Nigel on your own."

"Even if—"

"Those cats are despicable." Beau spat in the grass. "Promise me—"

"But, but, but," Tango sputtered.

Gently, Beau placed his paw on Tango's forehead. "Promise me that you will not go anywhere near the Pitiful Place."

"Okay . . . okay," Tango agreed reluctantly. "I promise."

CHAPTER 29

Without a Pack

A few nights later, Beau, unsettled and unable to sleep, ventured out of his den. The lights of the Cody house were blazing, the television blaring. Inside, the pack of children was rough-housing, shouting and laughing so loudly that Beau all but expected one of the little humans to tumble out of an open window. McKenna was in Miss Gustie's barn again, making candles.

Beau was worried about McKenna. Earlier, he'd heard a sweet tune wafting out of McKenna's stuffed bunny—a signal that she was deeply troubled.

Big Bart Cody and his wife, Jeannie, were sitting outside at the picnic table, talking. The tip of Jeannie's cigarette burned red. Wisps of smoke rose above whispered words that sparked into an angry exchange.

"Explain it, Bart," Jeannie demanded. "Explain it to me one more time."

Jeannie was a hard, brittle twig of a woman. Her voice was like stone scratching rock.

"I'm not going over this again, Jeannie," Bart said coldly. "I've told you what I know. Now drop it."

"McKenna is—or so she says—your sister's child?" asked Jeannie. "Pamela, who died in a car accident—ten, eleven years ago?"

"That's what I'm saying."

They were talking about McKenna! What concerned McKenna concerned Beau. He slipped between two lilac bushes near the picnic table.

"You'd never seen McKenna, not even once, before the night she showed up on our doorstep?"

"I told you, maybe once."

"When?"

"Let me see . . ."

Big Bart lit one of Jeannie's cigarettes. Now two reddish orange lights glowed in the dark. Beau took a couple of steps back, retreating from a swirl of smoke that had drifted uncomfortably close to his hiding spot.

"Little Art and I were both in the Coast Guard, stationed halfway to the North Pole. We got word that our sister married that bum, Lyle. Months before the wedding, Lyle and I'd had words—almost came to blows. Lyle was bad news—thought he was big stuff, with that fancy red Mustang."

Beau's stomach recoiled. The car that killed Tawny. Red and mean.

"I told Pam that Lyle was trouble. But would she listen? No. Next thing I know, we hear she has a kid. At her funeral, there's Lyle, carrying a black-haired kid who's screaming her head off. Then I met you. We got married. We moved to Victoria. I never heard from Lyle again."

If only Beau could speak the human tongue, he'd tell Big Bart the whole story. The real story. Somebody should know. Now that she was old enough, McKenna herself should know.

"McKenna's getting on my nerves. I think she's sneaky." Jeannie patted her belly. "Plus, we've got enough to worry about without her."

Bart raised his voice. "I told McKenna she can stay the summer, and if I say she can stay, she stays."

Beau let out a sigh of relief. Bart Cody, Beau sensed, was a gentle soul at heart, but he was no pushover.

"Somebody must be looking for her," Jeannie said.

Bart swung his leg over the picnic bench, stood, and crushed his cigarette butt into the ground. "We'll cross that bridge when we come to it."

To Beau's ears, it sounded like the kind of trouble that had followed McKenna ever since the woman in the red car, Pamela Skye, got killed.

Sighing, Beau sat back on his haunches. At times like these Beau felt very, very old—weary with concern for his beloved McKenna. So much had happened since she'd called out, "Hey, fox! I'm leaving! For good. You coming, or not?"

At the time, Beau had no idea that the confused, impetuous girl would journey any farther than she had before, when she'd run away from these human homes called "foster." Being raised by so many different people seemed unnatural, Beau lamented anew. In the fox world, adoption is lifelong, the bond permanent.

Saddened by the scene he'd witnessed in the Codys' backyard, Beau returned to his den. He'd always thought that if he followed McKenna around long enough, someday he'd see her in a place she could call home.

Up until tonight, Beau felt certain that McKenna had finally found her human pack, here in Victoria-by-the-Sea.

Now he wasn't sure.

CHAPTER 30

Trouble Brewing

When it came to McKenna Skye, Augusta felt like Hansel and Gretel, following a trail of bread crumbs. McKenna let slip pieces of information—Pamela Skye, an auto accident—as she and Augusta worked together to perfect the candle-making process (far more complicated now that McKenna insisted on stirring certain ingredients—heaven knows why— into the wax).

Was McKenna lying? Did she, in fact, know her birth mother's name? Had McKenna discovered where this woman now lived? Was it Toronto? Or was McKenna going there by herself, thinking that all her problems would go away once she lost herself in a big city?

One evening, McKenna offered Augusta a few more crumbs.

"Some county lady's been snooping around,"

McKenna remarked, offhandedly. "Big—I mean—Uncle Bart, acted like he hadn't seen me, but said if he did, he'd let her know."

"That sounds like something Bart Cody would do."

"Uncle Bart says he doesn't place much stock in government."

"Is that so?"

"She left a card. It's that Mrs. Gaspé. She's a social worker. I figured she'd have given up on me by now."

"And what about the Codys?"

"Jeannie says I can't stay. She doesn't like me."

"You're her husband's niece, for heaven's sake! Maybe you could help her more," Augusta suggested. "Take care of the kids, and—"

"Take care of those brats? No, thanks."

Later, inside her house, Augusta walked past the sepia portraits in gilded wood frames on her parlor wall. Her parents: born and raised here, her grandparents, too. All village folk, in the same house for over a century. Augusta couldn't imagine how adrift McKenna must feel. No roots. No deep soil.

The next morning, Augusta shared what she knew with Jack Tucker, and wouldn't you know it—he went ahead and did some checking.

A few days later, Jack stopped by in time for afternoon tea. Washing a bite of freshly baked shortbread down with a swallow of tea, Jack explained, "I was up in Queens County, anyway, vaccinating a flock of lambs, so I made a few stops, asked a few questions."

He handed Augusta a photocopy of a newspaper article from about eleven years earlier. Augusta skimmed the article: *A woman killed instantly . . . head-on collision . . . the causeway bridge . . . two survivors . . . a toddler . . . alcohol involved.*

The photo of the two mangled cars was gut-wrenching.

"My Lord, Jack, whatever you do, don't show this to McKenna. And what's this about a stuffed rabbit?"

"Seems the toddler—McKenna, if it really was McKenna—had the rabbit in her hand when they pulled her out of the wreck."

"Oh my gosh."

Jack pushed himself away from the table. "And there's more."

Augusta leaned down and pulled Pup, who was wearing the dark green knitted scarf, into her lap.

"As Priscilla tells it, a lady from Queens County was up at the post office asking where Bart Cody lived. She was looking for a girl named McKenna Skye—had Priscilla seen a girl by that name around? Seems that McKenna is a ward of the county—a runaway."

"Oh, my," Augusta murmured.

"Priscilla sent the lady Bart's way. When the lady asked Bart, he didn't exactly lie, but he didn't exactly tell the truth, either."

The bells above the shop door tinkled. Pup barked and squirmed out of Augusta's lap. Jack followed Augusta as she hurried out of the kitchen and into her shop, with the little dog in the lead.

Augusta waited patiently as a short woman pillaged through the sweaters and scanned the wool scarves. Nothing, it seemed, caught her eye. Then she pointed to Pup, now poised on the padded seat of the rocking chair.

The well-dressed woman fingered the fringe of the tiny scarf on Pup's neck. "Do you have any more of these? I assume you made it?"

"You mean his scarf? Yes, I made a couple, but just for him."

The woman plucked a business card out of her wallet. "I'll be back on the island next month. I'll take three dozen."

Augusta glanced at Jack, who had an odd smirk on his face. He flashed ten fingers.

Augusta's tone of voice was crisp and businesslike. "I'll need ten dollars per piece."

"Fine. It's a deal."

"I'll be doggoned," Jack said after the woman left the shop. He took Augusta's binoculars off a hook near the front door. "Looks like a New York license plate."

Pup jumped off the rocking chair. He bounced up and down, scratching at the screen door, trying to open it.

Augusta eyed the business card and handed it to Jack.

"Pandora's: THE Place for Pampered Pets." Jack grinned.

Augusta frowned, unable to get the disturbing newspaper story out of her mind. "Listen, Jack. Maybe I should call up there, find that social worker."

"It's none of your business, Augusta, and you know it. It's Bart Cody's business. He's the one who's sheltering McKenna. He'll handle it the way he sees fit."

"But Jeannie said that McKenna can't stay. There's no room. With a baby on the way, and half the kids living in the attic . . ."

Jack smiled down on the little dog, who was back in Augusta's lap. "So, what did you decide to name him?" he asked, changing the subject.

"If Pup's still here at summer's end, I'll name him. If no one's come by then, I guess they won't."

Pup sat up and stiffened. His black button nose pointed up and off to the side.

"Sometimes," Augusta puzzled, "I swear that Pup

understands every single word someone says . . . quite uncanny."

"For conversation's sake, mind you, what would you name him—if you were to name him, I mean?"

A long-ago memory caught Augusta unawares.

She'd been about McKenna's age. She'd written a report about dogs—dogs like King Edward VII's dog, Caesar; Ulysses' dog, Argus; and Grey Friar's Bobby.

Caesar—a terrier, Augusta recalled—had walked ahead of kings and princes in his master's funeral procession in 1910.

"Argus, Bobby, Caesar—what difference does it make?" Augusta griped. "He's not my dog."

Jack ruffled the fur on top of Pup's head. "What do you think, little guy, should we call you Caesar?"

"Don't be ridiculous."

"Anyway, back to McKenna. You know as well as I do: it's possible that half of what the girl says isn't true," Jack said. "These foster parents are checked out by the county. They're probably good people who have turned themselves inside out trying to help her."

"I don't think we know," Augusta half-heartedly acknowledged. "And, like you said, it's none of *my* business."

CHAPTER 31

Cat-and-Dog Dance

Tango couldn't believe his good fortune. The mystery was almost solved. His two pieces of silver had slipped off his neck when he slid into the sea. McKenna had the chain. Most likely, Nigel had the heart. McKenna Skye was the key to putting the pieces together.

Tango was sure she'd understand. Hadn't McKenna known exactly what to do when he expressed his desire to save the jellyfish, just as they had saved him?

Oh, what fun they'd had!

He'd race ahead, zigzag across the sand, and when he located a jellyfish, he'd bark. McKenna would skip, barefooted, over to where Tango was, and with her shovel, scoop the jellyfish into her bucket. At the edge of the sea, McKenna tossed the jellyfish back into its watery home. Sometimes, they found only one or two, but other days, ten, even twenty, jellyfish dotted the sand.

Deep in his soul, Tango understood how desperately the jellyfish wanted to go back to the sea and be reunited with their own kind. How proud his good, generous sister Theresa would be of her brother. His mother, too, Tango thought.

Doing his daily good deed, Tango temporarily forgot about returning to Marcellina.

∞

However, as July turned into August, Tango's desire to go back home returned with full force. Tourists were descending on Victoria-by-the-Sea like flies on a restaurant Dumpster in Manhattan. Both McKenna and Augusta were working from earliest morning until late into the night.

One afternoon, Tango asked Beau if he'd come up with a plan to get Tango's silver identification tag back from Nigel Stump.

"Nigel Stump is evil—at the very least, he's Axel's spineless pawn. Do not let your desire for the silver cloud your judgment."

On this unusually hot, windy day, Tango's loneliness was unbearable. His nose just inches from the sand, Tango wandered aimlessly up and down the narrow beach. Even the village children, diving off the wharf at high tide, were too busy to take notice of him.

Lost in thought, Tango didn't see that Nigel Stump was trailing him.

"Rat-Boy, my man, what're you doing? Looking for something?"

Tango was in no mood to be called Rat-Boy, especially by a surly, three-legged cat.

"Maybe."

"Maybe *I* could help you find what you're looking for. *I've* got experience," Nigel claimed arrogantly.

Beau's strict warning—*do not, I repeat, do not*—echoed in Tango's mind. But if Tango was smart about it, and Nigel just happened to tell him something, that wouldn't be breaking his promise, would it?

"Maybe you could," Tango replied. "I thought I saw something shiny in the sand just now, but I can't find it."

"A guy's gotta be pretty sharp to find the good stuff out here. Lucky, too."

"I bet you've got a real good eye, being so experienced and all."

Soaking in the compliment, Nigel's face softened. "It's all a matter of timing. When you see something, you can't hold back—you gotta take it and run."

Nigel threw his head toward the bay, where

white-capped waves glistened in the sun. "Listen up, Rat-Boy."

Tango flinched—he couldn't stand being called Rat-Boy.

"A guy can get busy out there, lose track of time. Before you know it, the tide rolls back in. If you get trapped on a sandbar, you're in BIG trouble."

Tango inhaled a breath of cool, crisp air. *Play it smart*, he told himself. *Ignore the put-down—stroke the cat's ego.*

"You know, the way you get around on three legs is pretty amazing—if you don't mind me saying so." Tango smiled.

"It takes practice, my boy." Nigel nonchalantly circled Tango. "So, you said you saw something shiny out here?"

"I'm pretty sure I did," Tango answered.

"Hmm, I'm pretty fond of the shiny stuff myself."

"You are? Like what?" Tango asked. "What's the best thing you've ever found?"

Nigel's pea green eyes shifted—from Tango to the Pitiful Place and then back to Tango. The cat's tail curled like a snake on the sand. "I probably shouldn't be telling you this . . ."

Tango's heart was pumping wildly. Hoping the cat wouldn't notice, Tango feigned interest in a sailboat moored at the wharf.

"A while back," Nigel whispered, "I found a silver heart."

"Really? A silver heart?" Tango nodded with
enthusiasm. Beau was right! Tango thought his body
would burst!

"Shiny as a star. I'm quite fond of it."

Slow down, Tango cautioned himself. *Play it
smart.* Flattery will get you everywhere, he remembered Diego once saying.

"A silver heart? Wow—you're good!"

Nigel licked his left leg, stopping at the spot
where his skin was hobbled and scarred.

"Like everyone says, Rat-Boy, Nigel Stump's the
best."

Tango's jaws were ready to snap. If they did,
Nigel Stump wouldn't be calling him Rat-Boy any
longer. But again, Tango held back.

"I'd love to see that silver heart," Tango murmured.

Nigel flicked his tail. The white hairs on its tip
brushed across Tango's nose.

"No way. No dogs," Nigel said. "Only cats allowed
in the Pitiful Place."

Tango was losing patience with this cat-and-dog
dance. "That's not what I hear."

Nigel's mood changed. He shoved his black-
bearded face into Tango's. "What, Rat-Boy? What do
you hear?"

"Oh, what I mean—what I meant to say—is that the Pitiful Place is where all the village animals hang out at night, right?"

"Private. By invitation only. Very exclusive." Nigel puffed out his chest. "But, listen, I'll talk to the guys." He twitched his whiskers. "I've got a little clout. Maybe I can get you in."

Tired of flattering the arrogant cat, Tango could contain himself no longer. "The silver heart is mine," Tango growled viciously.

Anger and frustration—a desire for what was rightfully his—overpowered him. Tango lunged at Nigel, closing his jaws just short of Nigel's throat.

The fur on Nigel's back exploded into a field of black needles. "Hey, hey, hey! Calm down."

Tango bared his sharp teeth. "And I want it back. Now."

"You say the silver heart is yours?" He pointed at one of Tango's footprints in the sand. "A little charm about that big?"

Like a shot, Tango drove his muzzle into Nigel's chest. Nigel stumbled backward over a flat sandstone rock.

"Back off, little buddy. Back off. There's a peaceful solution here. Listen up," Nigel said as he rolled out of his fall. "We've got a motto: All for one and one for all. Technically, the silver heart's not mine.

But, hey, I'm a reasonable fellow. I'll talk to the guys."

"When?" Tango demanded.

"Soon. But I gotta warn you—the guys aren't going to give up the heart just because you say it's yours. They're not fools. They'll want something in exchange."

He had the upper hand, and knew it.

Beau had been right—Tango'd been a fool. He'd opened his mouth and made things worse. Now Nigel was on to him.

"Something good—a fair trade." Nigel gave Tango a sinister grin. "When you come up with something, let me know. I'll arrange a little handoff. But you'd better hurry," Nigel warned. "Things at the Pitiful Place have a way of disappearing, if you get my drift. . . ."

"I get it."

Nigel turned and stuck his rear in Tango's face. "Later, Rat-Boy."

CHAPTER 32

Unlikely Heroes

Dawn was breaking. Heavy clouds hung low in the sky, blocking the light of the rising sun. The second of the summer lobster fishing seasons had begun; McKenna awoke to the grumbling of engines as the boats set out to sea. Unlike the first season, in early May, the second season started in mid-August with neither fanfare nor blessing.

Deep in thought, McKenna rolled her fingers across her silver ankle bracelet. She'd been in Victoria-by-the-Sea for almost four months. It was time to plan her move.

In the first light, McKenna studied a map. As soon as it was dark, she'd follow the rarely used red roads to Charlottetown. From there, she'd catch a bus, and then take a train.

She fingered the envelope with Annie Pike's address on it, hoping that Annie hadn't moved.

McKenna intended to show up on Annie's doorstep without warning. Caught by surprise, Annie wouldn't have the heart to turn her away—would she?

Her social worker had called Big Bart again to see if McKenna had contacted him. With a concerned look on his face, Big Bart handed McKenna a slip of paper. "Maybe it's time you make the call."

McKenna glanced at the Queens County phone number. "I will, Uncle Bart."

"Promise?"

"I'll call. I promise," McKenna told him. And she would, she decided—from a pay phone in Toronto.

"I'm sorry, McKenna. You can stay until the first of September and not a day longer. There's nothing I can do."

McKenna put the map into her pouch and pulled out a wad of dollar bills. The last two days she'd sold out of enchanted candles. If this kept up, she'd have enough money to take off by the end of the month.

Suddenly, McKenna heard a series of raspy barks. She pulled the pouch strings tight. The high-pitched yapping sounded as if it came from Miss Gustie's little dog.

McKenna shrugged. He was probably chasing a rabbit that had slipped through the fence. Or digging for a mole that dove into a hole.

The gritty barking continued, louder now, and more desperate.

McKenna pulled on a sweatshirt, shoved the pouch to the bottom of her sleeping bag, and jogged barefooted over stubbles of crab grass in the Cody backyard.

The barking intensified when Pup saw McKenna. As if knowing that he had her attention, Pup sprinted toward the steps in front of the mudroom door and then turned around, pawing at the ground.

Miss Gustie's kitchen light was not on. The familiar tail of smoke was not rising from the chimney. The teakettle wasn't whistling.

Something was wrong.

McKenna dashed to the door and rapped loudly. There was no response. She paused, not wanting to enter without permission. She peeked through the windowpane, but saw nothing but shadows.

"Miss Gustie! Miss Gustie?"

McKenna twisted the doorknob, opening the door a few inches. Pup darted inside.

Everything in the mudroom looked in order, but in the alcove off the kitchen, Pup started scratching viciously at a door in the floor, which McKenna had never noticed before.

"Darn it, dog. Stop barking, will you?"

A moan rose from beneath the floor.

"Pup, move! Quick!" McKenna shouted.

Pushing Pup aside, she pulled on the brass ring. The heavy door angled up and open. McKenna's fingers shook as she fumbled with the hook.

"I'm here," Miss Gustie cried weakly.

The slim daylight from the mudroom's single window barely illuminated the dark cavern below. A dank odor rose out of the darkness.

"Hang on, Miss Gustie, we're coming!"

McKenna looked for a light switch—somewhere, anywhere—but found none.

Suddenly Miss Gustie let out a scream. Pup scampered into the cellar, disappearing from sight.

Miss Gustie screamed again. "Get it off of me! Get it off of me!"

McKenna heard Pup yelping. Then a snap—a scuffle—a short, shrill whistling sound.

She grabbed hold of the handrail. "The light! The light! Where is it?"

Now Miss Gustie's voice was quiet but controlled. "Go down backward. Be careful. The bottom stair broke. Light chain's right above you." She paused, groaned, and then all but whispered, "Don't step on me."

Once she planted her feet on firm ground, McKenna pulled the light chain. A cone of light illuminated Miss Gustie's splayed body. Next to Miss Gustie's body was a smashed glass jar. Whatever had been in it was dark red and gooey and had splattered all over her bathrobe.

McKenna bent down and laid her hands on Miss Gustie's shoulders. "Geez, Miss Gustie, what did you go and do to yourself? It's practically the middle of the night."

Her face a chalky gray, Miss Gustie winced. Her breathing was labored.

"What hurts? Tell me where?"

"Couldn't sleep. Wanted jam." Miss Gustie gasped and rolled onto her side. "For my toast." Her teeth chattered. Her body trembled. "I'm so cold. So-so-so-cold."

McKenna scanned the cellar for something she could use to cover Miss Gustie. Pup whined loudly. McKenna looked in his direction.

"Gross!" McKenna cried out.

A brown wharf rat was laying at Pup's feet near Miss Gustie's outstretched hand. A tiny stream of blood trickled from the rat's mouth.

McKenna grimaced. She stood up, and with her bare foot, kicked the dead rat into the corner. Pup was about to go after it, but McKenna yelled, "No, Pup, NO!" and he backed off.

"Get help," whimpered Miss Gustie.

McKenna hoisted herself up to the second step. "Pup, STAY!"

McKenna scaled the remaining stairs. Something warm, something warm, she needed something warm. She ran to Miss Gustie's shop, grabbed an armful of sweaters, and sprinted back to the hole in the floor. She dropped the sweaters down onto Miss Gustie's body.

"Here, cover yourself up!" McKenna shouted. "I'll be right back."

Thoughts of how to get help scrambled in McKenna's mind. Big Bart was fishing. Doc Tucker lived in another town. With a shaking finger, she hurriedly dialed what she believed was the island's emergency number. "What city are you calling, please?"

Information! McKenna slammed down the receiver and redialed "0." When no one picked up after three rings, she left the receiver hanging on its cord and bolted out the door.

Priscilla! The postmistress would know what to do!

It took only seconds to rouse Priscilla, who responded to McKenna's strong-fisted pounding on her door in a bathrobe and pin-curled hair.

"I'll get help," Priscilla said. "Go back and wait in the front yard. Flag down the rescue squad when it comes. I'll tend to Augusta. Show them where we are."

To McKenna, it seemed like forever before the ambulance arrived. It took three men to hoist the stretcher up the steep stairs. Miss Gustie moaned and struggled against the pain.

Called out of their beds by a blaring siren, a crowd of villagers huddled near the One-of-a-Kind sign. As the stretcher passed, they quizzed McKenna with their eyes for an explanation of what had happened.

As the ambulance sped away, McKenna picked Pup up and held him over her wildly beating heart. "You did good, little dog. You did good."

How had Pup descended so steep a set of stairs so quickly? Had he jumped? And how had he killed that rat in such short order? The dog had always seemed so helpless.

"I didn't think you had it in you." She smiled.

Meanwhile, Priscilla had taken center stage in the circle of villagers. McKenna was relieved to have their eyes focused on somebody else. When the postmistress said "sweaters" and "jam" in the same sentence, McKenna's chin dropped.

The sweaters! Miss Gustie's beautiful, expensive sweaters! How could she have been so stupid?

As the wailing of the siren diminished, McKenna

stroked the downy, fawn-colored fur on the little dog's forehead. "I guess you and Miss Gustie are even. First, she saved your life, and now you saved hers."

∞

For two days, the "Closed" sign hung on the door of One-of-a-Kind. The uniquely beautiful sweaters and other woolen works of art sat untouched on the shelves. In the village there was a general consensus that Miss Gustie's shop must not close. Miss Gustie could ill afford to give up her bread-and-butter, even if she did dislocate her kneecap, break a few ribs, and fracture her hip going down into her cellar for jam.

However, when it came to finding someone to work in Miss Gustie's shop, every person in the village, it seemed, was already tied up with a sixteen-hour workday, seven days of the week.

On the third day of her hospital stay Miss Gustie made it clear to Doc Tucker, who made it clear to the rest of the villagers: McKenna Skye, if she was willing, was to manage One-of-a-Kind and continue to care for Pup, as well.

In hushed tones villagers questioned whether the young stranger could be trusted with such a great responsibility. Gossiping tongues flapped like the wings of gulls in flight. *Why, the value of Augusta's antiques alone . . . the expensive sweaters . . . all it would take . . . I heard it was raspberry . . . what is Miss Gustie thinking?*

When Jack Tucker got wind of it, he let it be known—in no uncertain terms—that he would take personal responsibility for Miss Gustie's decision. He'd also get the sweaters cleaned. The villagers were silenced.

By the very next day, One-of-a-Kind woolen works of art by Augusta Smith were being sold at Enchanted Candles from nine in the morning until three in the afternoon; and enchanted candles by McKenna Skye were being sold at Augusta's One-of-a-Kind from three in the afternoon until nine in the evening. The gate in the picket fence was always open.

But, sometimes, on evenings after McKenna closed up shop, Pup would curl up next to her on Enchanted Candle's whitewashed floor. McKenna would count the money—first, what belonged to her, and then what belonged to Miss Gustie.

She'd chew her fingernails and rub her forehead, thinking about foster homes and social workers and people getting paid to take care of her because no one really wanted her for real. She'd see herself sneaking out of the village, on her way to Toronto, with nothing but her backpack and loads of money.

She'd wait for her friend, the fox, to follow, but she knew, deep in her heart, that the fox would refuse. Then McKenna would look into Pup's eyes, aglow in the light of an enchanted candle's strong flame. She'd find her ragged bunny and slowly wind the key. When the Bun-Bun's lullaby ended, McKenna would spread all the money on the floor.

And there she'd sit, cross-legged—one bare ankle sparkling with silver—dividing what was hers, and what was Miss Gustie's, into two unequal piles—fair and square—exactly like Miss Gustie expected.

CHAPTER 33

Not for Sale

About a week after coming home from the hospital, in the quiet time between the dinner hour and the first act at The Village Playhouse, Augusta heard shouts coming from the direction of the Cody house. Loud sounds spilling out of her neighbor's house were quite familiar, so, at first, Augusta paid little attention. If the racket got worse, she'd close the windows.

Certain words, however, became louder and more distinct: "I won't go! I won't go! I'm not going, and you can't make me!"

Augusta rolled her wheelchair over to the bay window and pulled back the curtain. In the Codys' yard, a woman with a briefcase and a stern look on her face was speaking with Big Bart. At his side, McKenna appeared extremely agitated. Augusta tried to make sense of what she was seeing. Meanwhile,

Pup whined and whimpered and scratched at the front porch door.

"Mind your own business, Pup," she told the dog, but he didn't listen. When the front door wouldn't open, he made a beeline toward the back.

With a sinking heart, Augusta let the curtain drop, but as soon as she did so, the bells above her shop door jingled with urgency. McKenna burst into the house, to the small parlor, where Augusta was sitting with her hands clutched in her lap. Pup was not far behind.

"Miss Gustie, please! Please don't let them take me."

McKenna's charcoal eyes were wild with fire. Augusta felt weak in the face of such—such—what could she call it? Fear? Desperation?

"Please! She said I had to get my things and go with her NOW!"

Stay calm, Augusta told herself. *Weigh your words carefully*.

Augusta rubbed the deep creases on her forehead. "Who said?"

"Mrs. Gaspé! That social worker. She says that if I don't go with her, she'll call the police."

Augusta's insides were unraveling.

And, if the truth be told, Augusta's first thoughts were about herself.

How could she get along without McKenna's help? The girl had been a lifesaver—wouldn't accept a dime, insisted that helping others was the Mi'kmaq way.

Besides, Augusta fretted, what could a fusty old woman in a wheelchair do? A twelve-year-old girl, to whom she's not even related, begging her to intervene—how could she?—on top of her own fall? . . . No, no, it was all too much.

"Miss Gustie, please!"

The dog—well, with the dog, she'd acted on impulse, but McKenna was a child! No, not a child—almost an adolescent with needs and desires and expectations, and, and—

Augusta took a deep breath. "I'm afraid, my dear, that you have no choice. There are rules about such matters. The woman is only trying to do her job."

"Fine! Nice knowing you!" shouted the enraged girl.

The angry bells jangled. The door slammed. Augusta sighed, whatever words she might have wanted to say stuck in her throat.

"Oh, what are you looking at?" she asked Pup angrily. "It's none of my business—isn't that what Jack said?"

Augusta peeked through the holes in the lace curtain. McKenna's long hair was flying like a black flag as she ran down Main Street toward the wharf.

"Oh, my," Augusta mumbled.

Augusta thought that someone would have chas
McKenna. But there, at the picnic table, sat Big Bart
with his head in his hands. The social worker's hand
was poised on the door handle of her car. A little
row of Cody kids stood nearby—dumbfounded, it
seemed.

Augusta glanced at the dreamcatcher that hung
on the wall above a steel-framed medical bed that
was set up in the parlor.

A few days after Augusta complained that her
pain medication gave her nightmares, McKenna had
fashioned the webbed hoop out of green branches,
cotton string, strips of leather, colored beads, and
feathers. Truly, a work of art.

"Long ago, the spider gave his web as a gift to a
grandmother of our people, who'd saved his life,"
McKenna explained. "Now you'll remember only
the good dreams. Your bad dreams will get tangled
in the web."

Augusta hadn't had a nightmare since. She
reached for the phone and punched in Jack Tucker's
number. Who else could she call?

"There's nothing you can do, Gustie. Let go,"
Jack advised. "You've got enough trouble, eh? But if
you want, sure, I'll swing by."

When Jack showed up a few hours later, he
announced, "Big Bart got rid of the lady from the

as furious about being lied to. Didn't
.rt. He told her that McKenna had to stick
. Victoria long enough to close up shop before
. cleared out. He'd drive McKenna back to the
North Shore next weekend. The lady made him sign
some paper. Big Bart was steamed, I tell you."

"Then it's final? McKenna's going back into foster care? The Codys have decided against her?"

"For sure. Jeannie's dead set against it." Jack
adjusted the slide on his string tie. "But McKenna's
not going back into foster care. Mrs. Gaspé said
a foster home is no longer an option. She found a
place for McKenna in some residential school."

"Where? McKenna's going to leave the island?"

Jack shrugged. "What're you going to do? It is
what it is."

"Oh, those Codys."

"Come now, Gustie. That's not the right family
for a girl like McKenna."

He rolled up the sleeves on his plaid shirt. His
forearms were deeply tanned, his hands large and
strong.

"She's like that little dog of yours. She needs a
home where someone can give her the kind of attention she deserves."

Augusta raised her voice and spouted, "Why, Jack
Tucker, I certainly hope that you are not implying

that *I* take her in? Why don't *you* take her in? There's plenty of room in that big empty house of yours. She's good with animals. She'd be a tremendous help to you, I'd bet."

"I'm too old and set in my ways. You know that, Gustie."

"Well, it's not too late to change, I always say."

Jack glanced at his stainless steel watch. "Listen, I've got a bunch of sick cows to attend to." He took a folded square of yellow paper out of his shirt pocket and handed it to Augusta. "Here. In case you're interested."

"Hello! Hello! Are you open?" a woman's voice called as Jack let himself out.

Augusta slipped the yellow paper into her skirt pocket.

"Yes, I am," Augusta called. "I'll be right with you."

Augusta recognized the voice of the woman with the fancy pet products business. The woman made Augusta uncomfortable. She'd be glad to get paid for her work and get rid of her.

"Is my order ready?" the woman asked.

"Yes, indeed," Augusta answered as she rolled herself out to One-of-a-Kind by way of a small ramp with a slight incline that Jack had fashioned.

Blind to Augusta's obvious injuries, the woman's

blue-shadowed eyes were sparkling. However, she was not looking at the cardboard box overflowing with fringed woolen scarves for small dogs. Her sights were set on Pup, who was lying on the padded rocking chair.

"Oh, there's my boy!" Without so much as asking, the brassy blond woman lifted Pup and held the squirming dog out in front of her. "He's a Yorkie, right? Purebred?"

"That will be three-hundred and sixty dollars," Augusta said brusquely. "Thirty-six scarves at ten each."

"And how much for this precious, precious pooch?"

How much for the dog? Who did this woman think she was?

"The dog is not for sale," Augusta snapped.

The Pampered Pooch woman set Pup back on the rocker. She laid three hundred-dollar bills and three twenties on the table. "For the scarves."

Next to the small pile of bills, she put another hundred dollar bill. Then, as if she were dealing cards, the woman stripped four hundreds out of the wad of money in her hand. "Will you take five hundred for the dog?"

Augusta was aghast. "The dog is *not* for sale."

With an impassive face, the woman dealt a

second hand. Six hundred, seven hundred, eight hundred . . .

"The dog is . . ." Augusta paused, arrested by a vision of the sky-high stack of unpaid bills on her writing table.

Pup, with a slight quiver to his ears, sat upright, straight and tall, as if prepared to do battle.

The woman squeezed Pup's teacup face. "You are such a cutie! A perfectly perfect model. I'll put you in my shop window, and—"

She faced Augusta, looking like a Rottweiler who was used to getting her own way. "A thousand dollars for the dog," she offered. "Take it, or leave it."

Augusta steered her wheelchair close to the rocking chair and, grimacing, pulled Pup into her lap.

Augusta's strong, calm, and almost inaudible voice betrayed her rankled emotions. "No, thank you."

The woman scooped up the taller stack of bills. She laid down her business card. "In case you change your mind," she said smugly.

Once the impudent woman left the shop, Augusta's anger erupted. "Who does she think she is? As if I'd sell Pup to the likes of her!"

Augusta ripped the business card into tiny pieces.

Then she pulled the square of paper out of her skirt pocket. "Dorothea Gaspé, Social Worker," Augusta read quietly.

Another uppity woman who probably thinks she knows what's best for everyone. Her hands shaking, Augusta started to tear this paper as well.

Pup cocked his head to the side and gave her a quizzical look. Augusta caught herself before she went any further. "You're right, Pup. I'd better hang on to it, just in case."

With closed eyes, Augusta bowed her head, greatly relieved that she hadn't given into temptation and taken the money.

"Well, Pup, it seems I just bought myself a dog."

Finally, once and for all, Augusta acknowledged how much joy the little dog had brought to her once-lonely life.

"And a thousand-dollar dog deserves a fancier name than Pup."

Pup shifted his ears forward.

"Oh, and in case you're wondering, it's not going to be Caesar." She shook her head, chuckling. "Caesar and Augusta—can you imagine? What's wrong with that Jack Tucker? We'd be the laughing stock of the whole village."

Lying in the hospital, she'd had plenty of time to think. She'd also had time to reread Homer's *Odyssey*. Jack was right—*her* dog deserved a name. "Pup" wasn't nearly heroic enough—and didn't the little dog all but save her life?

Pup continued to stare at her intently. Augusta pictured the great adventurer, Ulysses, walking into the courtyard palace, dressed as a beggar, and Argus, his loyal dog, almost dead with age, recognizing his long-gone master with a glad tail, unable to rise.

"No, I'm not going to give you your new name quite yet. But I will."

She fluffed Pup's ears. "When it's time."

CHAPTER 34

A Fair Fight

Under the majestic oak tree in Miss Gustie's backyard, Beau nibbled on green acorns, the first to have fallen from the tree. The night breeze had a distinct chill, an early warning that summer was coming to an end.

As he waited for Tango, Beau recalled Tawny's scent, her sweetness, the soft white fur on the underside of her chin. With each passing day, Beau was more eager to join her.

Nagging concerns about his fellow animals in the village, particularly his friend Tango, interrupted Beau's reverie. Tango hadn't told Beau right away about his encounter with Nigel Stump. When Beau asked why, Tango reminded Beau that he'd been busy since Augusta came home from the hospital. McKenna was counting on him to keep watch.

"Don't get your hopes up," Beau had cautioned. "Surely you are not so naive as to think that the cats will simply turn the charm over to you."

"They want something in exchange. What do you think I should give them?"

"Tango, whatever you offer will not be enough. Don't be deceived. Others have been—with grave consequences."

Recently, Beau and some of the animals had successfully banded together to warn others not to accept Nigel Stump's "invitation" to a "party" at the Pitiful Place. Beau's allies reported that Old Ada's deserted house had been silent for three straight nights. Now their leader, Axel, was pressuring not only Nigel, but also the other cats, to "come up with some action."

Beau shook his head. Where was Tango? Surely Miss Gustie was asleep by now. If the little dog did not appear soon, Beau would head for the freshwater creek to find some crayfish for his supper.

In the distance, waves rumbled as they broke on shore, but above the sound of the sea, a voice called in the night.

"Hey, Rat-Boy!"

Beau's body tensed.

"Hey, Rat-Boy! Where are you?"

Confident that he smelled a cat from the Pitiful Place, Beau asked, "Who wants to know?"

"It's me, Nigel Stump."

With his distinctive three-legged gait, Nigel hobbled out of the shadows, across Miss Gustie's compost pile.

Suddenly, swoosh! From atop the picket fence, another cat pounced onto the ground, almost landing on Beau's tail. Beau spun around and snapped at the cat's ears.

"Take it easy, old boy," Nigel cautioned. "It's only Briar."

"The dog—whose name is Tango, by the way—is not here."

"Too bad. The mutt seemed pretty anxious to get his silver heart back. We've been waiting to hear from him."

"So you do have the charm," Beau said.

Nigel chuckled crassly. "Well, about the charm— let's just say that there's been a slight change in plans."

When the copper-eyed Briar snickered, Beau snarled back. The twilight blue cat hunched her back and hissed.

"Let's not mince words," said Nigel. "I have a message for the Rat-Boy. See that he gets it."

"His name is Tango."

"Like I was saying, if Rat-Boy wants his silver heart, he's going to have to take it away from Malachi. In a fair fight."

"What does a big white rat want with a piece of silver?" Beau challenged. "It makes no sense."

"You see, sweetie," Briar explained, "Malachi's been locked up as punishment for vandalizing our hangout, but we proposed a deal. If he takes down Rat-Boy in three rounds, Malachi gets his freedom. If not, Rat-Boy gets the charm, and that nasty, nasty rat gets what he deserves."

Beau spat in disgust.

"We're spreading the word," Briar said. "Anybody who's anybody is going to be there."

"What makes you think Tango will agree to such a fight?" Beau asked.

Beau recalled Tango's fright the night they encountered Malachi for the first time. Tango was no match for a rat who was bent on revenge.

After the hair-raising incident at the lighthouse, Beau had done some checking. He discovered that after Old Ada died, Malachi was the only rat to have survived the purge. The glass and steel-barred cages inside the Pitiful Place were gruesome reminders of the way Malachi and his fellow rodents had suffered. Malachi hated the house. He also hated its current inhabitants.

189

No, Tango would be mercilessly slaughtered.

"If Rat-Boy wants his heart back, he has no choice." Briar smirked.

"Where, exactly, is this supposedly fair fight going to take place?"

"The Pitiful Place," Nigel said. "Come early if you want a ringside seat. In fact, we'll save you one. You seem to be the only friend the dog has." Nigel paused. "Oh, but you'd better warn Rat-Boy that Malachi's been sharpening his teeth on nails. Tell him: Beware the teeth. Beware the tail."

Where was Malachi imprisoned? Beau wondered.

"I'm so excited," Briar mewed. "A little dog fighting a big rat. Should be ver-r-ry interesting."

"I beg to differ," Beau said. "The fight will not be interesting. Tango is a city dog, domesticated and naive—completely unfamiliar with the ways of the wild. Your so-called entertainment will be over in the blink of an eye."

Nigel and Briar exchanged worried glances.

"I offer myself as a more equal opponent."

Briar snickered. "You? You, old fox, are one step away from the grave."

"Not so fast," Nigel cautioned Briar.

"I may be old, but size and cunning are on my side," said Beau.

"The fox could be right," Nigel said. "Maybe we should check with Axel."

Suddenly, with a swish of branches and a rustling of leaves, a small, compact animal sprung out of the bushes. Beau's heart jumped. Briar gasped.

Tango! Teeth bared and fur standing on end!

"I can fight my own battles!" the little dog declared.

"Well, well, well," Nigel said. "Speak of the devil. . . ."

"Tango, no, listen to me," Beau implored.

Tango ignored Beau and fixed his eyes on Briar. "So, what's the deal?"

"Tango, there is no deal," Beau said.

"If I take down Malachi in three rounds, the charm is mine?"

Tango had overheard the entire exchange! In the old days no animal could have ever come so close without Beau's knowledge.

"It's all yours, Ratty-Boy," Briar answered.

"Tango, just because you killed a small brown wharf rat, do not assume—"

Nigel rudely interrupted. "There's nothing left to talk about. Malachi versus Rat-Boy. Tomorrow night."

"Tomorrow night," agreed Tango.

Beau had lost his taste for acorns.

While Tango watched in silence, Beau paced back and forth. Did the little dog have any idea what his foolhardy act was going to cost him? Tango was no match for a gigantic, crazed, starved rat. Even if Tango won, would the cats keep their promise? In his heart, Beau knew the answer. Beau also knew that the foolish little dog wouldn't listen.

Beau's pacing became more labored. Feeling old and defeated, Beau turned toward Enchanted Candles.

Barely audible, Tango asked in a small voice, "You're not mad at me, Beau, are you?"

Mad? No, Beau was not mad; Beau was tired. Tired of creatures that could not live in peace. Tired of waiting, waiting, waiting for the Great Sky Spirit to call him Home.

"No, I am not mad. It's just . . ." Beau hung his head. "Forgive me, Tango, but tonight I cannot endure your hope; I can only endure my own despair."

"What are you trying to say?"

Beau did not answer. Wearily, he retraced his footsteps back to his foxhole beneath McKenna's shed, where he would cradle himself in the comforting smell of the sweet red clay.

"What do you mean, Beau?" Tango called into the night. "What do you mean?"

CHAPTER 35

The Final Storm

Throughout the next day, villagers would remember, the weather on the south shore of Prince Edward Island had been temperamental. At sunrise, thick mist hovered over the bay. The sea was as still as glass. When the mist cleared, the sun was hot, intermittently covered by bloated clouds. Late in the afternoon, strong winds from the southwest churned the frothy waves.

Tango, too, had been temperamental. Tonight's fight with Malachi weighed heavily on his mind. Beau was right: Malachi was no small wharf rat, like the kind he'd killed in Augusta's cellar. And, in truth, ending the brown rat's life hadn't felt nearly as heroic as all the humans made it out to be.

But it was too late now.

Spurred on by the desire to get his charm back, Tango plotted his strategy, devising ways to avoid

Malachi's razor-sharp teeth and whiplike tail. Taking Malachi down, and keeping him down, was no small challenge. But that is exactly what Tango would need to do to win back his silver charm.

Soon the wind doubled in strength. Young trees bent in its path. Brittle branches snapped. By the time the bold red sun dropped out of sight, the winds were nearly gale force. Tourists took to their cars. Villagers closed their windows and awaited the storm.

Augusta, exhausted by sporadic attempts to walk with a three-footed cane, was fast asleep on the sofa. Earlier, Augusta told Tango that she was sick and tired of being impaired. She missed the little things most, like hanging wash on the line, weeding her garden, mowing her lawn.

Now it was time for Tango to go to the Pitiful Place. In case he never saw Augusta again (for fear filled his heart), he tip-toed across the afghan covering her body. He'd never had a chance to say goodbye to Marcellina. He allowed himself a moment to linger, licking the hand that had petted, brushed, bathed, and fed him.

Half-asleep, Augusta opened her eyes. "You know, Pup," she mumbled. "If I didn't have you around to keep me company, I don't know what I'd do."

Her eyes were clear and deep as tide pools. If Tango dove in, he would drown.

Augusta reached back over her head. "My medicine—now where is that?" She searched the end table with her fingers. "What time is it? Oh, my. Pup—get McKenna for me, will you? Good dog."

As he'd done so many times since Augusta had fallen down the cellar stairs, Tango ran out to the picket fence. As loudly as he could, Tango barked the bark that told McKenna that Miss Gustie needed something.

"All right, already!" McKenna shouted over the wild, whistling wind. "Tell Miss Gustie to cool her heels! I'm on my way."

Tango felt a lump in his throat.

McKenna, Beau had told him, was also leaving— in a day or two. Big Bart was driving her back to the North Shore. After both Tango and McKenna were gone—assuming he recaptured his silver heart and Marcellina came for him—who would care for Augusta until her hip healed?

But what could Tango do? He was only a dog.

Tango shook off his concerns, imagining instead the money that Marcellina would shower on Augusta. A lot more than a thousand dollars, he'd bet. With all that money, Augusta could hire people to take care of her: a nurse, a maid, a cook, a driver.

What tugged at Tango's heart even more was that Augusta was planning to announce his new name tomorrow. Jack Tucker was bringing a bakery cake to celebrate. McKenna was making an enchanted candle with a base of red sand scooped from the exact spot on the beach where Tango had washed ashore.

Augusta drifted back to sleep. Tango took his leave in silence.

As planned, he met Beau inside his den.

"Beau, can I talk to you about something?"

"Of course."

Tango told Beau that he was worried about abandoning Augusta.

"I understand. A dog cannot have two masters," responded Beau. "Nor can you prevent Miss Gustie's pain. It is too late for that. You have won her heart. She has claimed you as her own. Miss Gustie's devotion to you is stronger than bonds of silver."

Tango frowned at the truth of Beau's words. He had to stay centered; he had a job to do.

As Tango and Beau pressed forward into the bullish night, the wind all but ripped the fur off their backs. The sea was gaining strength, a thunderous swooshing as waves bashed against the shore.

"Please, Tango," Beau pleaded. "Will you not reconsider? I fear for your safety. These winds are harsh and unforgiving, warning us to turn back."

"Wait, I'd better warm up."

Trying his best to brush off the fear the fox's

words were instilling, Tango stretched his body, flexed his muscles, and ran in a circle to warm up. He snapped his jaw and imagined his teeth sinking into Malachi's neck.

"Truly, Tango, I do not like the sound of this. The sky is angry."

"How bad can it be?" Tango questioned.

The one-hinged door to the Pitiful Place swung open. Leftie, the orange cat with the twisted smile, braced the door and motioned with his head for the two canines to come forward.

"I guess we will soon find out," Beau answered.

CHAPTER 36

Power Outage

Fighting the raging wind, McKenna Skye headed to Miss Gustie's house. With a drumroll of sustained thunder, the heavens split open. A hurricane lantern swung in McKenna's hand, but cold pellets of rain instantly doused the flame.

For the fourth time that summer, the village's power was out. Earlier in the day, Priscilla had dropped off a tuna casserole and apple pie for Augusta and McKenna's lunch. Out of Miss Gustie's earshot, Priscilla compared this summer's storms to that freak season some thirty years back, when Albert Smith, Augusta's husband, smashed his lobster boat against the rocks near Slade's Cove.

After she got Miss Gustie settled in for the night, McKenna planned to replenish her candle stock. Enchanted or not, her candles were selling well. McKenna had repaid Doc Tucker in full and still had almost eight hundred dollars in her pouch—more than enough to get her to Toronto. A couple more days, and she'd be gone.

Earlier in the day, Big Bart had reminded McKenna that he'd be driving her to Mrs. Gaspé's office first thing on Monday morning.

"When I turn on the engine, you better be packed and in the truck, McKenna," he'd said. "Don't mess this up. I don't need any more trouble."

Soon, McKenna knew, she wouldn't be giving anyone on Prince Edward Island any more trouble.

With the wind at her back, McKenna burst through the barn red door on the water side of Miss Gustie's house. Once inside, she tried to relight the lantern, but the wet wick wouldn't burn.

From her bed in the parlor, where she was propped against a pillow, Miss Gustie beamed a flashlight in McKenna's direction. "This storm is going to be a doozy!"

"It already is!"

Miss Gustie turned off her battery-operated radio. "Nothing but static."

"Should I make you a cup of tea before I go out back?"

"Go out? This is no night for man or beast to be out. They're expecting winds up to ninety miles per hour. We'll be lucky if my little barn doesn't fly off its foundation with you in it."

"Speaking of beasts, where's Pup?"

"Oh, he's around here somewhere." Miss Gustie's eyes narrowed. "I think. Find him for me, will you?"

"I'll need some light."

Miss Gustie handed McKenna the flashlight, yellow and square, with a black plastic handle. "Here, take this."

McKenna searched every nook and cranny of the house. She lifted the door to the cellar, even though she knew there was no way Pup could be down there.

"I can't find him anywhere," McKenna reported back.

"What do you mean, you can't find him? He has to be around here somewhere! Did you check out back? Maybe his doggie door got stuck."

"Yes."

"How about the—"

"I've checked everywhere, Miss Gustie. Trust me. He's not here."

Even in the dim light, McKenna could see the color drain from Miss Gustie's face. The creases in her forehead deepened. Her hands formed taut fists.

Miss Gustie pulled back the bedcovers and shifted her legs, as if a woman with a fractured hip and dislocated kneecap could get up and search for Pup herself.

"He can't be far," McKenna said quickly. "Have you got another flashlight?"

"No, take this one. I'll light my candle. But you'd better put on my rain slicker. It's hanging in the mudroom."

McKenna's sweatshirt and jeans were clammy and cold, but she had no time to change. She'd better get going, or Miss Gustie was going to have a heart attack. McKenna hoped that Pup was either sheltered in the barn, or down in the fox's tunnel. McKenna thought she'd seen the two canines together earlier in the evening, but that was something she'd better not share with the already panicked woman.

She put on the black rain slicker and came back to Miss Gustie's side. "If I find Pup out in the barn, we'll stay there until the storm passes. Don't worry—I'm sure that's where he is. He's probably too scared to come out."

McKenna stepped back into the storm. The winds howled as if in pain. Trees screamed as branches were ripped from their limbs.

Inside the barn, raindrops hammered the roof. McKenna beamed the flashlight across the floor, in all the corners, inside the dory, and even on the rafters, where a pair of snowy white barn owls perched. McKenna called and called his name, but the little dog didn't come running.

She rolled the barn doors shut. Head down, pushing through sheets of rain, McKenna made a mad dash to the back side of Enchanted Candles. She dropped down on her knees and called into the fox's tunnel.

"Pup! Pup! Come out of there! Miss Gustie's worried sick. Fox, you send him home now, you hear?"

Again, there was no response. Were Pup and the fox still together? If so, where?

The lighthouse? Maybe, but she'd seen Big Bart bar the door; McKenna couldn't get in even if Pup were inside.

The wharf? No, she'd never seen the little dog hang out anywhere near the wharf. The only other place she could think of was the Pitiful Place, where those nasty wharf cats lived. That place gave her the creeps. She wouldn't go inside—not alone— but the minute the storm let up, she'd take a quick look, just in case.

When she tried to stand up, McKenna slipped on the wet mud and fell down, facefirst, in the mire. Deafening thunder shook the earth beneath her feet.

KA-BOOM! A jagged bolt of lightning cut across the sky. McKenna screamed, pressing her hands over her ears.

KA-BOOM! The second bolt of lightning struck, closer, much closer. An imagined bolt of sizzling electricity traveled up her spine.

McKenna knew she had to seek shelter. She tried to prop herself up, but her elbows were shaking, and she couldn't make them stop.

Suddenly, it was a rainy night in April, and she was running, running, running away from Mr. Z.— his hands, his anger—running, running across the island. No idea where she was going, knowing that she had to get away; she had to get away.

KA-BOOM! The thunderous crack of a third bolt of lightning snapped her body into action. McKenna wiped the wet mud off her chin and bolted to the doorway of her shed. She pressed her body within the door frame, under the eave, but even there, the slanting sheets of needling rain found her.

Drenched and shivering, she gripped the wet doorknob with trembling fingers. She dug her frozen fingers into her jeans pocket, feeling for the key.

Then, from behind her, came an eerie, drawn-out wail followed by a series of short, raspy barks. McKenna's heart stopped. When she turned her head, the fox's blazing amber eyes were fixed on her own.

Later, McKenna would swear that the fox had said something to her, something like, "Follow me."

Maybe he did. Maybe he didn't.

In any case, at that moment, when, with a grand sweep of his rain-soaked tail, the fox turned and ran at top speed toward the Pitiful Place, McKenna knew exactly what she had to do.

CHAPTER 37

In the Ring

Giant rolling waves battered the south side of the Pitiful Place. Tango and Beau climbed up the rickety ramp that led from the street to the door. Leftie led Tango and Beau across its threshold. The ancient stilts, which secured the structure onto its rocky foundation, creaked and quaked as if about to break.

Inside, strikes of lightning gave the interior intermittent moments of light. The Pitiful Place, Tango realized, was more than pitiful. A ghetto of glass and wire cages, many broken or bent, filled most of the living space. Stacks of newspapers looked like misshapen skyscrapers about to fall. Books were strewn about, pages torn, bindings broken.

A sickening stench rose from a pile of open cans, bones, trash, trash, and more trash. Tango gagged, pressing his paw across his nostrils to block the rancid odors.

Tango searched the ghoulish space for Nigel. He didn't see the keeper of his charm, but what he did see astonished him.

Twenty, thirty, maybe forty animals were gathered in a loose semicircle on the fireplace side of the large room. Moles, voles, squirrels, rabbits, chipmunks, skunk. A pair of weasels. A beaver.

"Don't worry, my son," Beau whispered to Tango. "They are on your side."

"Why? They don't even know me."

"They know *of* you."

"I'm not sure I want an audience."

"Tonight, they're witnesses to evil. But after, perhaps they'll join together to fight it. Even if you . . ."

Tango shuddered. "Even if I what?"

"Even if you do not succeed, your courage will light the way for others."

Near the brick fireplace, Axel and Tate, bold and fat from too much feasting, strutted about. Briar, Leftie, and Flint were pressing their bodies against the door of a beat-up refrigerator. Someone, or something, inside the refrigerator was pounding and scratching.

When he couldn't locate Nigel, Tango had an appalling thought: What if Nigel was lying? What if there was no winner, no loser, and no silver prize? What if there was another reason why he and

Beau and all the others had been lured into this hellish pit?

Tate, the all-black cat, tapped on the refrigerator door. "You can come out now, Mal. Your victim is here."

The three cats stepped aside and let the door drop open.

Collectively, the animals flinched at the sight of Malachi: a creature they'd heard about but few had actually seen. Framed in the refrigerator's pale interior, the giant rat's eyes glowed like red-hot coals. His lower body was puffy and misshapen, and from his shoulders to his ears, growths and tumors packed his fur.

"I'm done for," Tango moaned.

Malachi clumsily stumbled out of his confinement, but quickly got his bearings. Then, stroking his whiskers and licking his chops, the albino rat pinned his beady eyes on Tango.

A loud, scratchy voice called for the animals' attention. Nigel, posted atop the fireplace mantle—with no charm in sight—shouted, "Let the games begin!"

As shrieking winds circled the outer walls of the Pitiful Place, inside, Tango heard a thumping, soft drumming sound: *Tango, Tango, Tango.*

Looking over his shoulder, Tango searched Beau's face.

"Remember: you are fighting for all of us," said Beau, with a touch of pride in his voice.

Beau was wrong, Tango cried silently. He was fighting for himself: fighting for his silver charm and his chance to go home.

His heart pumped wildly. Tango took a few tentative steps forward. Malachi opened his jaws wide, like a trap, and displayed four long, yellow teeth.

Tango's eyes darted around. Finally, he caught a glimpse of Nigel, the silver heart clamped in his brownish teeth. Angry and emboldened, Tango's feral spirit sparked.

Louder and louder, in unison, Victoria's creatures—eager for the fight to begin—chanted: *TANGO! TANGO! TANGO!*

Tango took deep breaths, inhaling courage. Trying not to look at his hideous opponent, Tango silently chanted mantras.

You are strong, you are brave, and you are fearless.

You are Apollo, Zeus, Rex, Spike.

Your ancestors, the brave terriers of Yorkshire, line up in pride behind you.

You are THE TANGO!

Screeching and gnashing his teeth, Malachi tried to push his way out of the ring that the five cats had formed around him, but the cats tightened the circle, preventing the rat's escape.

"You have youth and wit on your side," Beau advised. "Use both, and you will prevail."

Tate and Flint made an opening for Tango to pass through. Once Tango was inside the makeshift fighting ring, Malachi bowed slightly—a small moment of dignity that cast the rat in an entirely different light.

Malachi held up a front paw, signaling a desire for silence. When he opened his mouth to speak, every animal inside the Pitiful Place hushed.

"Little dog, whatever happens, I bear you no grudge. You and I are nothing but innocent pawns in the cats' sinister game."

The cats responded with spits and hisses. Pawn or no pawn, all Tango wanted was to get his charm and get out. He scraped his front paws across the wood floor, anxiously waiting for Malachi to make the first move.

The fear that had been choking Tango loosened. When Malachi didn't attack, Tango shouted, "On guard!"

Tango sprang into the unprotected soft spot beneath Malachi's chin.

In response, Malachi spun like a hurricane, hurling Tango down with his bare tail. When Tango tried to stand, Malachi's long tail sliced like a blade beneath Tango's feet. Tango stumbled. Whatever strategy he'd dreamed up was worthless in the face of the monstrous rodent.

Beau, who stood just outside the cats' circle, motioned for Tango to come close. "Tango, you must wear him down. Keep him spinning."

Malachi's tail lashed out a third time. Tango danced back and forth, inviting Malachi to knock him down, which is exactly what the leathery whip did a third, then a fourth, then a fifth time.

Finally, Tango caught the rhythm. Soon he was jumping over Malachi's tail like a child skipping rope. The cat pack jeered; the small animals of the field and forest cheered Tango on.

The dreadful dance continued. Foam covered Malachi's jaws, and wads of spit showered Tango's body. Back and forth, back and forth, Tango leaped and retreated, leaped and retreated.

With each attack, Tango got closer to the spot he was going for. With one perfect move, Tango could hop on Malachi's back and sink his teeth into the rat's spine. If he failed, he'd go for Malachi's neck.

Suddenly wild and out of control, all Tango wanted was to finish Malachi off.

On his next attack, Tango's teeth drove deep enough into Malachi's neck to draw blood. Beneath their feet, the floorboards groaned. With the bitter taste of blood now on his tongue, Tango saw the image of the brown rat he'd killed in Augusta's basement. In his mind, the dead rat asked: *Is the silver charm worth killing for?*

The ancient house rocked and swayed. Tango felt dizzy and confused, seasick and sick at heart, as if he were once again riding the swells of the violent sea in Diego's sailboat. Panicked, Tango looked around. Eyes wide with fright, all the animal spectators were scurrying away. Malachi stepped back, as if unwilling to attack.

And Beau? Where was Beau?

The Pitiful Place lurched. Malachi lost his balance, and the rat struggled to right himself as seawater streamed under his feet.

Tango saw his chance. One final lunge, that's all it would take. Tango prepared to spring.

Above them, the furious wind ripped at the roof. Tango heard the sound of splitting wood and shattering glass.

Suddenly, a split-second vision of his mother's face appeared—at that long-ago moment when Tango had dangled at the end of Mr. Bailey's fingers. A tear was dripping from each of Sadie's sad, brown eyes. She, too, seemed to be asking: *Is the silver charm worth killing for?*

Was it? Panicked and uncertain, Tango searched for Beau—wanting, desperately needing—his friend.

Malachi's tail smacked him in the legs and he toppled. The large rat sprang, pinning Tango's squirming body to the floor.

Eager for the albino rat to finish the little dog off, the bloodthirsty cats whistled and cheered.

Later, this is what Tango would remember: he would remember the rat's body transforming into an amorphous cloud of hazy white fur. He would remember four golden, glowing spikes inside Malachi's smile. He would remember Malachi saying, "No, little dog, it is not," as if answering an unasked question, before the rat slipped out of sight.

CHAPTER 38

Betrayed

The seas heaved. The Pitiful Place moaned and groaned. With his strong hind legs, Nigel tried to stabilize himself on the fireplace mantle, while every force of nature wanted to hurl his crippled body into the chaos below.

Just when Nigel thought that Rat-Boy was about to finish Malachi off, the dog hesitated. Malachi pounced on his opponent. Grinning repugnantly, Malachi bared teeth capable of chewing through lead pipe—a feat that Nigel had witnessed.

But no, Nigel couldn't watch. He *wouldn't* watch. He could only close his eyes, waiting for the little dog's death scream.

Unexpectedly, Malachi let out a hideous laugh. Nigel took a quick peek. In the blink of an eye, the rat slapped Briar in the face, and then slithered into the fireplace, up the flue, and out of sight.

Cat calls and insults spun around the room.

Quickly, Axel, Tate, Leftie, and Flint surrounded Rat-Boy, preventing the dazed dog's escape. The four cats were wild and out of control, oblivious to danger. When Leftie and Flint leaped to the fireplace mantle, Nigel let out a sigh of relief. His two buddies must have sensed Nigel's fear, and they were scrambling up to help him get down. Flint shimmied close to Nigel's left side, Leftie to his right.

Nigel heard a vicious chuckle and felt the pressure of four cat paws on his back, and then a hard shove. Nigel flew off the mantle, too stunned to scream. His three legs spread like useless wings. He landed on his stomach with a *splat!*

Nigel couldn't comprehend what had just happened. When he looked up, he saw a halo of ten cat-eyes, a constellation of misguided stars.

Suddenly, the little dog's body landed on top of him, and Leftie was shouting, "Go get him, Stumpy-Boy!"

"He's all yours, Stump, sock it to him," Flint whooped.

They were expecting *him* to fight Rat-Boy!

Lightning hit the roof. Window frames split. Shards of glass bulleted through the room. With a thunderous rumble, the southwest corner of the stilted structure began to give way. The next thing

Nigel knew, the dog was gone, and slimy seawater was soaking his skin.

Nigel didn't care. He had no intention of getting up.

He'd wait for the waves to wash him away. He'd been cruelly betrayed—by his best friends, his only friends.

Just before he closed his eyes, for what he thought was the last time, Nigel saw a train of cats' tails heading up the stairs to the second floor. Axel was in the rear. With a pity in his eyes that Nigel had come to despise, Axel looked back at Nigel. With his paw, Axel motioned Nigel to follow him.

But Nigel was done following. He'd rather die than go where Axel was leading.

The floor tipped. Rat-Boy's body slammed into Nigel's, feeling more like a boulder than a ball of dog. Entwined, their bodies slid across the fireplace hearth and rolled into the blackened firebox. With a resounding crash, the queen's chair fell on its side in front of the opening, blocking any chance for escape.

Shaking with a common fright, the little dog and Nigel huddled together while the Pitiful Place rocked back and forth.

A sob rose up from someplace deep in Nigel's gut, and his teeth unclenched. Just inches away, the little dog's brown eyes lit up.

Momentarily, Nigel took comfort, knowing that before his own life ended, he would return the silver heart to its rightful owner. Nigel dropped the charm. For a split second, the thin piece of silver spun on its rim, then Rat-Boy snapped the silver between his teeth.

The waves roared. The wind screeched. And above it all, Nigel heard Malachi laughing, laughing, laughing—the sound of the unforgiving rat's revenge.

CHAPTER 39

Set Free

Blinded by rain, McKenna followed the fox across Water Street, past the wharf, to the stilted house once occupied by Old Ada Phillips and dozens—maybe hundreds—of mice and rats. The beam of Miss Gustie's flashlight illuminated the entrance where the door was banging in the wind. Amazingly, through this doorway, down the ramp, out every window, small animals with wild eyes ran, jumped, hopped, and tumbled.

McKenna wiped her wet hair out of her face. "What the heck is going on?"

The fox darted into the grisly house.

McKenna crossed the threshold, steps behind the fox, only to be assaulted by a putrid stench. The house was swaying as the waves surged beneath the floorboards.

"Hurry, Fox!" she shouted. "Find Pup! We've got to find him!"

Lightning crackled. Glass shattered.

"Pup! Pup! Are you in here?" McKenna beamed the flashlight around the ghoulish room. "Pup! Pup! You're in here. I know you are!"

Outside, a huge wave slammed against the Pitiful Place and splashed into the room. McKenna fell against a stack of cages, which toppled on others that had already fallen.

"Bark! Pup, do *something*! I can't see you!" she screamed as she struggled to right herself.

"Yip-yip-yap-eee! Yip-yip-yap-eee!"

McKenna steadied the beam until the light found the yelping fox's silvery tail. More waves surged below the boards where McKenna stood. Somewhere above her, timbers cracked as the structure lurched. "Fox, hurry! This place is going down!"

Finally, a high-pitched wail rose above the crashing, smashing, sliding sounds all around her. Near the fireplace, on top of an armchair that had tipped on its side, the fox screamed feverishly.

"Did you find him? Did you find him?"

Thunder rumbled like a fast-approaching train. Balancing herself with outstretched arms, McKenna moved toward the fireplace, crushing the trash in her path. Seawater streamed across the tips of her boots.

The fox jumped off the tipped chair. The wailing

continued. McKenna tried to drag the chair away from the fireplace, then lunged forward and draped her body over its broad arm. She shined the light into the hearth.

There, huddled in the corner, were Miss Gustie's little dog, Pup, and the three-legged cat, just out of her reach. They were trembling, their faces stricken with terror. McKenna stretched her arm until her fingers could almost touch Pup, who stared at her with wide, pleading eyes.

"Come here, Pup. Easy now," McKenna coaxed, trying to still the quake in her voice. "You, too, cat."

Again, the structure shifted. The animals slid in her direction. McKenna dropped the flashlight to free her other hand.

She groped wildly, feeling for fur. She needed two legs: one dog's and one cat's. She grabbed, hoping for the best.

When each of her hands had gripped a limb, she took a deep breath, and with a grunt, pulled and straightened her back. She drew the animals—there were two!—close. The cat hissed and spit, but Pup's body was limp.

The swift-running water was now ankle-deep, while a whooshing sound rose out of the sea, a deafening, dangerous moan.

Where was the door? She turned one way,

stopped, and then spun around in the opposite direction. Finally—it seemed like forever—she spotted the fox's glowing eyes, beckoning her forward.

McKenna stumbled toward the fox, followed him out the door, down the slippery, water-sodden ramp just as the Pitiful Place broke free. Standing back from the rocky shore, McKenna watched in awe as unrelenting, angry waves pounded the structure until it collapsed into the sea.

Now there was loud shouting. A number of shadowy figures, some carrying lanterns, were running down Main Street.

McKenna wanted no part in explaining anything to anybody. Clutching the animals, she took off, back to her shed. At the doorstep, winded and dripping with cold sweat, she lowered the three-legged cat to the ground. She unlocked the door and dove into Enchanted Candles.

McKenna spilled Pup onto the floor. She held the door open, giving the frightened cat a moment to decide whether he was coming in, or staying out. A few feet away, the fox watched as the black-and-white cat slunk into the shed, and then slipped away. McKenna pulled the door shut.

She felt her way to a shelf, searching for a glass jar that held books of dry matches. She struck a match and moved to the bench where a row of enchanted candles were waiting to be named. Fingers shaking, she lit one.

McKenna dropped to the floor, exhausted. She'd pull herself together, she decided, and take a few minutes to catch her breath. Then she'd head over to Miss Gustie's. McKenna closed her eyes, already beginning to doubt whether what had just happened was real.

The sopping-wet dog climbed over her left side and curled himself into the curve of her body. The three-legged cat crouched in the corner and yowled.

Pup nuzzled his wet snout against McKenna's chest. Suddenly, she heard something small, like a coin, drop to the floor. Pup wiggled out of her arms.

McKenna took the burning candle from the bench and held it close to Pup. The enchanted candle's flame illuminated a small, silver heart on the whitewashed floor. With cold, stiff fingers, McKenna picked up the charm. Holding it close to the flame, McKenna read the word printed on one side: *TANGO.*

Engraved on the other side were four tiny lines of print: a name, an address, and a telephone number. It was an identification tag, a silver identification tag for an animal named Tango.

With the little dog watching her every move, McKenna stripped off her boots, rolled up her jeans, and turned down the cuffs of her wet socks. She untied the strip of leather that tied the two ends of her silver ankle bracelet together and held the silver heart up to the small ring that hung on the last link.

The little dog nosed the charm and barked excitedly.

"Tango," McKenna murmured incredulously. "Your name is Tango."

CHAPTER 40

Not One but Two

Propped up by pillows in her bed, Augusta waited, unable to fathom why it was taking so long to find Pup. The worst of the thunderstorm had passed and Augusta still had a roof over her head. But where was McKenna? Where could she—where could they—be?

The flame of the enchanted candle was the only light. Fervently, Augusta prayed for McKenna and Pup's safe return. Then, for good measure, she held the enchanted candle and made a wish.

Bang! The side door burst open.

"Thank goodness." Augusta sighed, pressing her hands to her cheeks. McKenna! Who else could it be?

Augusta held the candle up. McKenna stood, silent, in the doorway. The rain outside was soft and steady now, gentle-sounding. In the dim light,

Augusta still could not tell whether Pup had been found.

"Well?"

Water ran down the rain slicker and leather boots squished as McKenna walked toward Augusta's bedside, unfolded her arms, and handed Augusta a wet, ratty-looking Pup.

The fishy-smelling dog squirmed up Augusta's chest and licked her face. He snuggled against her neck, settling himself into Augusta's hug. She was so relieved that the little dog had been returned, Augusta temporarily forgot his rescuer, until McKenna's chattering teeth finally caught her attention.

"My heavens, girl, you are soaked to the bone. Take off those wet things, quickly, and get yourself dry."

As Augusta commanded, McKenna dropped the slicker in a heap on the wood floor, then pulled off her rain-soaked boots, and peeled away water-logged socks.

They would leave a puddle, but Augusta had no heart to scold the girl. McKenna's wet hair hung in black strings, like the licorice Augusta loved as a child. Funny, Augusta pondered, the things that come to mind at a time like this.

"On second thought," Augusta said, "go upstairs, and take a hot bath. There's a robe on the hook. Hurry—or you'll catch your death."

The clock chimed twelve times, a new day.

"Take the candle. It's all the light we have."

Augusta paused, searching for words that could express the deep gratitude she felt. Only the most simple came to mind.

"And McKenna—"

McKenna glanced over her shoulder. "Yeah?"

"Thank you."

"Uh, sure thing, Miss Gustie."

Augusta sat in the dark fingering Pup's damp fur. McKenna's footsteps were slow and steady as she trudged up the staircase. Augusta heard the creaky hinges of her bathroom door as McKenna opened it, the turn of the brass handles on her bathtub, the running of water. These common house sounds, made by someone other than herself, were foreign to Augusta's ear, and at the same time, completely familiar.

Nestled in Augusta's arms, Pup warmed up. When McKenna came back down, Augusta would surprise her. She'd tell McKenna that she'd decided to name the Yorkshire Terrier after Ulysses' dog, Argus.

When McKenna asked why (since Augusta was certain the name would have no significance to McKenna), Augusta would direct McKenna to the bookcase. She'd ask McKenna to draw out Homer's *Odyssey*. They'd drink hot tea, and Augusta would read the classic story aloud.

But when McKenna came down and curled herself into the armchair near Augusta's bed, it was McKenna, not Augusta, who had a story to tell. And not just one story, but two.

CHAPTER 41

The Truth Hurts

At first, when McKenna told Miss Gustie that she'd discovered Pup—as well as a bunch of cats and dozens of small, wild animals—inside the Pitiful Place, Miss Gustie didn't believe her.

"Why, that's impossible."

Augusta had an even harder time believing that Old Ada's sad gray house had split apart and washed out to sea.

It would not be until the next morning, when the strange occurrences of the storm-filled night were the talk of the village, that Augusta would truly believe McKenna's story. By that time, rumors were spreading, including one started by Big Bart Cody. He swore that when he'd searched the bay with the wharf's emergency, long-range lantern, he'd seen four, maybe five cats clinging to the roof of Old Ada's house as the receding tide carried the roof out to sea.

The second story was one that McKenna had held inside herself for so long that her words should have spilled out rapidly, mixed with tears and emotion.

Instead, McKenna told her story in a voice as steady as a boat rowed on a windless day. And Miss Gustie listened, as much with her eyes as her ears.

"My real mother abandoned me."

"Your birth mother, you mean."

"No note. No nothing. Left me, in the middle of the night, cold and naked, on Pamela Skye's front lawn."

"I see."

"Wrapped in a fishnet."

Miss Gustie's eyes registered shock, but she didn't interrupt.

"I was only a couple of days old."

"Oh, my."

"After Mrs. Gaspé caught me reading the report last winter, she decided that a half-truth was worse than the whole truth, so she told me everything she knew."

"And, you say, this was later proven? That Mr. Skye was not your father?"

"I guess that's why he was so eager to get rid of me."

Augusta fell silent. She rubbed her chin,

momentarily deep in thought. "And where does Bart Cody fit into all of this?"

"The report said that Pamela Skye was a Cody. She had two brothers, once in the Coast Guard, who lived in Victoria-by-the-Sea."

"You mean Big Bart and Little Art?"

McKenna nodded. She squeezed her stomach. She didn't feel like talking about it anymore. "What difference does it make?" She glanced at the clock. "It's late. I'd better be getting back."

Miss Gustie's voice was firm. "No. Go on. It's important. You were saying that the Codys . . ."

McKenna sighed, allowing a deep breath of air to escape. "Big Bart and Little Art were at sea when the car accident happened. I went from one foster home to another. After Mr. Z. knocked me around, I headed in this direction. But one night, I took a wrong turn. When I saw that big blue sign for Victoria-by-the-Sea out there on the highway, it was getting late, and I was cold and really hungry. So I walked into the village. I asked this kid who was skateboarding on the wharf if he knew any Codys, and he pointed to their house."

"So Bart Cody isn't your real—I mean, blood—uncle."

"No, but I guess he thinks he is."

"It was good of him to take you in."

"Yeah, I know."

"How sad," Augusta said. "How terribly, terribly sad."

The little dog was cradled in Miss Gustie's arms, fast asleep.

Better to quit now, McKenna thought, before she had the chance to say anything else. She would put the silver heart on the chain and take Tango's identity with her to Toronto. She'd leave tomorrow night; it was her last chance.

But wrapped in Miss Gustie's robe, in the warmth of a candlelit room, McKenna's heart was heavy, her feet felt anchored to the floor. She was so, so tired. She guessed she'd just sit there for a little while longer.

McKenna closed her eyes, but soon the picture of herself as a baby, netted like some unwanted creature pulled from the sea, returned.

McKenna opened her eyes, shaking her head to scare off the image.

Miss Gustie was watching her. "You must forgive your mother, McKenna. She was probably very young."

"Yeah, so . . ."

"Very young, very afraid, and very alone—an act of desperation, I'm sure."

McKenna rested her head on her hand. "Miss Gustie, do you think my mother's ever been sorry?"

"I'm quite certain your birth mother has felt more sorrow than either of us could ever imagine. I'm also certain that you gave Pamela Skye more joy than you know."

"Really?"

"Truly, that's what I believe."

McKenna shrugged. "I don't know. Maybe."

"Really," Miss Gustie said. "But now, we must go to sleep. Mother always said that, no matter what happens, things will seem better in the morning. 'Sleep on it,' that's what she always said."

McKenna didn't know whether she could sleep on Tango's story any longer. If McKenna didn't tell Miss Gustie now, she never would. Wasn't everyone always telling McKenna to tell the truth? Wouldn't Miss Gustie *expect* her to tell the truth?

"Well, now you know, Miss Gustie, why I have to show you what I'm going to show you."

"What in the world are you talking about?" Augusta looked tired and confused. "Show me what?"

McKenna uncurled her legs and put her bare feet on the floor. She bent down and removed the silver link chain from her ankle. The little dog opened one eye, watching her every move.

"Miss Gustie, look." McKenna laid the silver links on the end table, right next to the enchanted candle.

Miss Gustie gave the chain a blank stare.

231

"Now look." McKenna took the small, silver heart out of the bathrobe pocket and laid it next to the chain.

Augusta squinted at what McKenna was trying to show her. McKenna demonstrated how perfectly the silver heart could be connected to the silver chain, and how easily the silver heart could slip out of the ring that once held it secure.

Then McKenna handed the heart to Augusta, who brought the charm close to her face. "Tango," Augusta read.

At the sound of his name, Tango squirmed, his eyes widening.

"Pup had this silver heart in his mouth—when I found him."

Augusta turned the charm over. "It's some kind of identification tag."

"I know," McKenna said, wondering how long it would take Miss Gustie to put two and two together.

Pup crawled over Augusta's body. The little dog seemed intent upon sniffing the pieces of silver.

"But . . . but . . ."

McKenna wrapped the chain around the little dog's neck. "See, it's a perfect fit."

"No, I don't see," Miss Gustie responded.

How could she not? McKenna wondered. It was so obvious!

McKenna dangled the chain in such a way that Miss Gustie *had* to see the truth. "The clasp must have broken when Pup washed ashore. That day, on the beach, you know—in the lobster trap."

Suddenly, the little dog lost interest in the silver charm and chain. He focused his eyes on the enchanted candle's burning flame, seemingly entranced by the candle's light.

"Don't you understand? It's a dog collar and tag."

"No," Augusta snapped, looking off to the side. "I don't understand."

Miss Gustie didn't want to know the truth. McKenna sighed, shook her head, and moved to the end of Augusta's bed.

McKenna broke the dog's concentration. "Tango?"

The little dog cocked his head.

"Tango!" McKenna called.

The dog's ears perked. And then, without the slightest hesitation, the dog now known as Tango scrambled away from Augusta, straight to McKenna, his docked tail wagging as much as a docked tail can wag.

CHAPTER 42

Sleeping on Silver

Now, McKenna Skye's stories were not the kind of stories that Augusta Smith wished to be told. The retired schoolteacher put her hands over her face. She would not, she could not, believe what McKenna was trying so hard to tell her.

To be sure, Augusta had never been the kind of woman who hid from the truth. So finally, when her mottled hands dropped into her empty lap, Augusta did what she knew she had to do, what she must do.

Augusta patted the bedsheet right next to her hip. "Tango," she called.

Just like that, the little dog left McKenna's side and plopped down in the exact spot that Augusta had patted.

Augusta's heart sunk. Oh my, the little dog wasn't Pup, or Nipper. He wasn't a Caesar or Ulysses. And he'd never answer to the name Argus.

His name was Tango. Like the dance.

Much to her surprise, Augusta started to cry. And what you need to understand is that when a woman hasn't allowed herself a good cry in an extraordinarily long time, the tears are very big.

"I'm sorry, Miss Gustie," McKenna said, her eyes glazed with tears. "I really am. But don't you see—I *had* to show you the charm."

McKenna proceeded to explain, stumbling on her words. "Tango's real mother—his real owner, I mean—gave him this heart. And even if he's just a dog, a dog belongs with the person who chose him." McKenna's voice raised a pitch. "You understand, don't you? You're not mad at me, are you? You wanted to know his real name, didn't you?"

With a tissue, Augusta wiped her cheeks and blew her nose. "No, no, of course not. I'm not mad. You did the right thing. It's just, it's just . . ."

"You got pretty attached to him, didn't you?" McKenna's shoulders slumped. "Yeah, I know. Me, too."

Augusta rubbed her eyes. "I couldn't see that well without my glasses. Where is Tango from?"

McKenna answered, "New York City."

"And his owner?"

"Some lady with a fancy name."

How in the world, Augusta puzzled, did a little

dog from New York City get tangled in a lobster trap in the Northumberland Strait?

Augusta would soon find out, it seemed.

Augusta squinted at the Baby Ben clock ticking away next to the enchanted candle. It was two o'clock in the morning. The enchanted candle's wax had melted considerably. If the flame wasn't blown out soon, the hot wax would flow over the edge of the candleholder and leave a pool on the furniture. Oh, what did it matter?

Augusta felt unbelievably tired and undeniably sad. Maybe because she was old, and maybe because she'd been lonelier than she'd ever been willing to admit, at this moment, the loss of the little dog seemed worse than losing Albert—worse than losing her mother.

"Miss Gustie, are you okay? Are you going to be all right?"

Augusta didn't respond.

McKenna buried her head in her hands. Oh, how could Augusta comfort McKenna when she didn't know how to comfort herself?

Augusta hugged the terrier now known as Tango and placed him in a cozy spot next to her pillow. "Normally, I don't approve of dogs sleeping in people's beds," Augusta told the little dog. "But since tonight might be one of your last nights in Victoria, I suppose it won't do any harm."

Tango rested his head on the edge of Augusta's pillow. He seemed perfectly at home—as if he'd been sleeping there all of his life.

"You go on upstairs, McKenna. It's too late to go back outside, even if the storm has ended. You can sleep in the room on the right at the top of the stairs."

"I don't know if I should. I left that three-legged cat in my shed."

"That black-and-white one? The poor thing's probably never had it so good. He'll be there in the morning, mark my words."

As Augusta bent over and blew out its flame, she wondered if the candle might possibly be enchanted.

If it was, Augusta knew exactly what she would wish for.

McKenna hadn't moved.

"Go on up now, McKenna. It's time."

In the dark, Augusta reached across the nightstand, and with the tips of her fingers, searched for the silver heart. Feeling like a child who'd lost a tooth, Augusta slid the silver heart under her pillow.

"Mother always said I should sleep on it, and that's just what I'm going to do."

Small, silent tears touched her cheeks. "Good night, Tango," she whispered. "I'll see you in the morning."

CHAPTER 43

Rooted to the Red Earth

Now you would think that Tango would have slept luxuriously in Augusta's bed. Wasn't he exhausted from his duel with Malachi, the big white rat? Wasn't his heart full of relief now that McKenna had made the connection between the silver charm and the silver chain that he'd once so proudly worn as a collar? Hadn't his wish come true? Wouldn't he soon be back in the arms of his mistress, the beautiful Marcellina?

Yes, Tango should have slept like a—well, like a dog.

But Tango did not.

Something in his life had shifted.

Tango couldn't believe how connected he could feel to someone, animal or human, who called him by his given name.

"Tango? Your name is Tango?" McKenna had

asked, but in such a way that it was not a question but a statement of fact.

"Of course your name is Tango," she'd said. "You look like a Tango. You act like a Tango. The name fits you to a T."

No suit of clothing, no costume, no disguise—his name sufficient, a perfect fit.

Oh, our little dog was troubled. Because while McKenna and Augusta had been exchanging the truth about who he was, Tango had seen something, brief and brilliant, in the enchanted candle's burning flame.

Inside the flickering light, Tango saw the glowing face of his beloved Marcellina. Marcellina held a Yorkshire Terrier, like Tango, except smaller and younger. The dog was wearing a tuxedo—not black, but white.

When Tango blinked his eyes, he saw something else. Now Diego stood by Marcellina's side holding a dog who looked exactly like his mother, Sadie, wearing a crown of tiny white roses.

What if the candle truly was enchanted? What if it was a warning—that he should not return to Manhattan?

Manhattan: harried humans, crowded streets, and dogs on leashes.

Oh, how Tango hated leashes! How he despised

dog walkers, who never let him go in the direction he wanted.

But it was more than people and streets and leashes.

If he went back to Manhattan—and he most certainly would if Augusta called Marcellina—he'd never see Beau again. His old friend—Tango choked up inside—would die alone. Without Tango, who would comfort the fox?

And how precious he must be to Augusta, the thousand dollars she'd been willing to give up to keep Tango—the sacrifice she'd made. Earlier, the way Augusta had cried.

And McKenna. Her sad story. Her broken heart. Beau Fox, who never left her side, her silent warrior, ever hidden, but always near.

Oh, he was miserable. But what could he do?

Dawn was breaking. Augusta would soon awaken. She'd make the call early; she'd want to get it over with.

Memories of Esperanza, Dulcinea, and Theresa returned. And it was then that Tango felt the seeds of hope. He felt the kind of power that had taken him to the top of the lighthouse and the kind of courage it took to fight for what rightfully was his.

Tango was not a little dog—not any longer.

Gently, carefully, Tango nuzzled under Augusta's

pillow. His rescuer was in a deep sleep, her chest rising and falling. Slowly, Tango pawed until the tips of his claws touched the silver heart, and, without waking Augusta, he scraped at the charm until it was close enough to clench in his teeth.

After springing through his doggy-door, Tango trotted across Augusta's rain-soaked grass. In the corner of her yard, between the rhubarb leaves and the raspberry bushes, Tango dug into the island's red clay soil.

The digging was slow. Water dripped off leaves and soaked his skin. While he worked, Tango felt the loving eyes of the old fox watching him, warming him, blessing him.

By the time the first ray of sun slanted across his back, the hole was deeper than Tango's body was tall.

With a tinge of regret and a touch of remorse—for Tango loved Marcellina and always would—he dropped his silver heart into the hole. He kicked the loose dirt back into the hole with his hind legs. Tango walked back and forth across the soil until it was packed as well as he could manage.

When he was finished, Tango turned and searched for his friend's silver-furred face, but the fox had taken his leave. Above him, a Great Blue heron flapped its wings—*shush-shush-shush*—and a white-tailed rabbit who'd been at the Pitiful Place hopped past, wiggled her nose, and whispered, "Thanks, Tango."

Soaked with sweat and drops of last night's rain, Tango didn't need a mirror to tell him that he resembled a very wet, very dirty, very large rat.

But the sun was rising. It was the time between tides.

Time enough to dip his body into the sea. Time enough to return to Augusta before she realized that he'd ever been gone.

EPILOGUE

Marcellina LaTour and Diego Cruz were married on a sun-filled December day at high noon, when diamond-bright snowflakes fell softly from the sky.

An article in the Weddings section of the newspaper described the ceremony in great detail. The matron of honor, Sadie, wore a crown of tiny white roses. Her son, Pierre, bedecked in a white silk tuxedo, acted as the official ring bearer.

The article described the members of the bridal party as "unusual" given that both Sadie and Pierre were Yorkshire Terriers.

A week after the wedding, one thousand miles north of Manhattan, McKenna Skye opened an issue of a celebrity magazine. McKenna showed her foster—soon to be, adoptive—mother, Augusta, a picture of a famous fashion model named Marcellina LaTour, and her new husband, Argentinian filmmaker Diego Cruz, flanked by two Yorkshire Terriers dressed in wedding attire.

Absentmindedly petting the three-legged black cat that she'd named Blackbeard, McKenna said, "Look at this, Augusta. Yorkshire Terriers—just like Tango."

Marcellina LaTour?

For a split second, McKenna paused, trying to remember when, or where, she'd seen this fancy French name before.

She shook her head. She hadn't—it was just her imagination.

Later, the Yorkshire Terrier now known as Tango would walk across Marcellina and Diego's wedding photo, on the end table, where McKenna had left the magazine lying open.

With the Prince Edward Island sun shining down on the glossy page, it seemed to Tango to be a perfect place to take a delicious nap.

And so he did, his heart at peace, at last.

ACKNOWLEDGMENTS

Without the wisdom and encouragement of two outstanding teachers, Sheila O'Connor and Jane Resh Thomas, *Tango* could not have been written. I am deeply grateful to these generous and gifted writers.

I would also like to thank my amazing agent, Linda Pratt, for believing in me, my work, and *Tango* from the very beginning; my skillful editor, Melanie Cecka, for giving *Tango* a loving home at Bloomsbury; and my mother and very first editor, Marcella, who gave me a 1935 edition of *Anne of Green Gables* when I was a girl, fueling my dream that somehow, *someday*, I'd write a book.

Also, many thanks to the many supportive friends and fellow writers who helped me find ways to tell *Tango's* story better, particularly Rosemary Davis, Joanne Esser, Wendy Jerome, Amy Schwantes, and Donna Studer.

Thanks also to the people of Prince Edward Island who have so graciously shared their province with me, my friends, and family for more than twenty summers.

Finally, to my husband Ralph; our children, Erin, Britt, Jonathan, and Janine; our grandchildren, Tadhg and Naoise; and the pets who have loved us (Angus, Gretel, Leftie, Louise, Sniffles, Tango, Tootie, and Watson T. Cat): You are the best. And when I say the best, I mean THE BEST.